Samuel French Acting Edition

The 39 Steps

Adapted by
Patrick Barlow

From the novel by
John Buchan

From the movie of
Alfred Hitchcock
Licensed by ITV Global
Entertainment Limited

And an original concept by
Nobby Dimon and Simon Corble

SAMUELFRENCH.COM   SAMUELFRENCH.CO.UK

FOR PRODUCTION ENQUIRIES

UNITED STATES AND CANADA
Info@SamuelFrench.com
1-866-598-8449

UNITED KINGDOM AND EUROPE
Plays@SamuelFrench.co.uk
020-7255-4302

Each title is subject to availability from Samuel French, depending upon country of performance. Please be aware that *THE 39 STEPS* may not be licensed by Samuel French in your territory. Professional and amateur producers should contact the nearest Samuel French office or licensing partner to verify availability.

MUSIC USE NOTE

Licensees are solely responsible for obtaining formal written permission from copyright owners to use copyrighted music in the performance of this play and are strongly cautioned to do so. If no such permission is obtained by the licensee, then the licensee must use only original music that the licensee owns and controls. Licensees are solely responsible and liable for all music clearances and shall indemnify the copyright owners of the play(s) and their licensing agent, Samuel French, against any costs, expenses, losses and liabilities arising from the use of music by licensees. Please contact the appropriate music licensing authority in your territory for the rights to any incidental music.

IMPORTANT BILLING AND CREDIT REQUIREMENTS

If you have obtained performance rights to this title, please refer to your licensing agreement for important billing and credit requirements.

In addition, the following credit must be given in all programs and publicity information distributed in association with this piece:

THE 39 STEPS

Adapted by Patrick Barlow

From the novel by John Buchan

From the movie of Alfred Hitchcock

Licensed by ITV Global Entertainment Limited

And an original concept by Simon Corble and Nobby Dimon

THE 39 STEPS was first produced on stage by North Country Theatre in April 1996 at the Georgian Theatre, Richmond, North Yorkshire. It subsequently toured extensively throughout the UK courtesy of Charles Vance. This latest version, adapted by Patrick Barlow from an original concept by Simon Corble and Nobby Dimon was first performed at the West Yorkshire Playhouse on June 17, 2005. The original UK production was directed by Fiona Buffini.

The original London production of *THE 39 STEPS* by arrangement with Edward Snape for Fiery Angel Limited, opened at the Tricycle Theatre in Kilburn on August 10, 2006 and transferred to the Criterion Theatre in the West End on September 14, 2006 with the following cast and creative team:

RICHARD HANNAY . . . . Charles Edwards
ANNABELLA SCHMIDT/MARGARET/PAMELA . . . . Catherine McCormack
CLOWN 1 . . . . Simon Gregor
CLOWN 2 . . . . Rupert Degas

Director – Maria Aitken
Designer – Peter McKintosh
Lighting Designer – Ian Scott
Sound Designer – Mic Pool
Movement Director – Toby Sedgwick
Casting Director – Simone Reynolds

THE 39 STEPS was subsequently produced by the Roundabout Theater Company, (Todd Haimes, Artistic Director; Harold Wolpert, Managing Director; Julia C. Levy, Executive Director; in association with Bob Boyett, Harriet Newman Leve/Ron Nicynski, Stewart F. Lane/Bonnie Comley, Manocherian Golden Productions, Olympus Theatricals/Douglas Denoff and Marek J. Cantor/Pat Addiss; and the Huntington Theater Company, Nicholas Martin, Artistic Director; Michael Maso, Managing Director; and Edward Snape for Fiery Angel Limited) opening on January 15, 2008 at the American Airlines Theater, directed by Maria Aitken with the following cast and creative team:

RICHARD HANNAY . . . . Charles Edwards
ANNABELLA SCHMIDT/PAMELA/MARGARET . . . . Jennifer Ferrin
CLOWN 1 . . . . Cliff Saunders
CLOWN 2 . . . . Arnie Burton
Costume and Set Design – Peter McKintosh
Lighting Design – Kevin Adams
Sound Design – Mic Pool
Original Movement Created by – Toby Sedgwick
Additional Movement Created by – Christopher Bayes
Stage Manager – Nevin Hedley
Production Management – Aurora Productions
General Management – Rebecca Habel and Roy Gabay

THE 39 STEPS subsequently transferred to the Cort Theatre on April 29, 2008 and the Helen Hayes Theater on January 21, 2009 and was produced by Bob Boyett, Harriet Newman Leve/Ron Nicynski, Stewart F. Lane/Bonnie Comley, Manocherian Golden Prods., Olympus Theatricals/Douglas Denoff, Pam Laudenslager/Pat Addiss, Tim Levy/Remmel T. Dickinson in association with Roundabout Theatre Company (Todd Haimes, Artistic Director; Harold Wolpert, Managing Director; Julia C. Levy, Executive Director) and the Huntington Theatre Company (Nicholas Martin, Artistic Director; Michael Maso, Managing Director) and Edward Snape for Fiery Angel Limited. General Management – Roy Gabay.

My grandfather, John Buchan, would be amazed and delighted that a play of his novel, *The Thirty-Nine Steps*, is being published as a script nearly a century after he wrote it for his own amusement. JB was never proprietorial about his work – for example, he loved the 1935 Alfred Hitchcock film of the book – and the more people who feel they want to put on and perform what was possibly the first spy thriller, the more delighted he would be.

On a serious note, two themes JB was anxious to convey in his novels were, firstly, that the veneer of civilization is very thin, easily exposing the horrors beneath and, secondly, that evil comes in very attractive forms, making it all the harder to resist. So the leader of the Black Stone gang in the book (Professor Jordan in the film and play) is urbane, cultured, charming and established in British country life – to such an extent that Hannay cannot believe he is evil. Despite the deft and funny way the action in this marvellous script by Patrick Barlow is portrayed on stage, those themes are not lost. I think my grandfather would have been very proud.

Deborah Buchan, Lady Stewartby
Scotland: July 2009

ADAPTER'S FOREWORD

This version of *The 39 Steps* is based on John Buchan's ground-breaking novel, Alfred Hitchcock's iconic movie and the exquisite idea of two Northern English writers Nobby Dimon and Simon Corble of doing the whole thing with just four actors. Our hero RICHARD HANNAY played by one man throughout. PAMELA, ANNABELLA and MARGARET played by one woman. And all other parts (I estimate a cool 250) played by two men called CLOWN 1 and CLOWN 2.

I have included most of my original stage directions and scenic ideas that I wrote before the play went into its first production in 2005. While it would be good to keep to the text on the page (much of it is from the original Hitchcock screenplay), I would certainly encourage adventurousness and flexibility in staging. Don't be bound by the instructions on the page. Just take what looks helpful or fun then invent the rest.

One of the thrilling things about writing this was the challenge of putting an entire movie on stage - complete with train chases, plane crashes, shadowy murders, beautiful spies, trilbied heavies, dastardly villains with little fingers missing, not to mention some of the most iconic moments in the history of cinema. There is much opportunity for comedy and satire here. But it's also a love story. A man and a woman who have never loved anyone, yet miraculously - through all the daredevil feats and derring-do – discover the beating of their own true hearts. That there's a reason to live and a reason to love. And above all a reason – as our hero (fired up by love though he doesn't know that's what it is yet) blissfully realizes in his passionately impromptu political speech – to look after each other and look after the world.

> *'Let's all just set ourselves resolutely to make this world a happier place! A decent world! A good world! A world where no nation plots against nation! Where no neighbour plots against neighbour, where there's no persecution or hunting down, where everybody gets a square deal and a sporting chance and where people try to help and not to hinder! A world where suspicion and cruelty and fear have been forever banished! That's the sort of world I want! Is that the sort of world you want?'*

Words written – remarkably – in 1935 by one of Alfred Hitchcock's team of writers and as resonant today as they were then.

As someone said the finest comedy comes from the greatest truth. Or was it the best comedy is deadly serious? Or was it play it for real and not the gag (that was Buster Keaton).

Anyway, whoever said what when, I'd respectfully ask you to remember the story too.

It's there behind the mayhem.

Patrick Barlow
November 2009

CHARACTERS

(If cast with 4 actors)

Richard Hannay
Annabella Schmidt/Pamela/Margaret
Clown 1
Clown 2

ACT ONE

Overture

(The actors run on and take a bow. Then frantically pull on the set for scene one.)

(Lights change.)

Scene One. Hannay's Apartment. London.

(In the centre of the stage is a large armchair, a standard lamp and a table. On the table a half empty bottle of scotch and empty glass.)

(Seated in the armchair is **RICHARD HANNAY**. *About forty. Attractive. Pencil moustache. He addresses the audience.)*

HANNAY. London. 1935. August. I'd been back three months in the old country and frankly wondering why. The weather made me liverish, no exercise to speak of and the talk of the ordinary Englishman made me sick. I'd had enough of restaurants and parties and race meetings. No pal to go about with – which probably explains things. Hoppy Bynge lost in the Canadian Treasury, Tommy Deloraine married off to a blonde heiress in Chicago, Chips Carruthers eaten by crocodiles in the Limpopo. Leaving me. Richard Hannay. Thirty-seven years old, sound in wind and limb. Back home. Which was no home at all if you want to know. Just a dull little rented flat in West One. Portland Place actually. And I was bored. No more than bored. Tired. Tired of the world and tired of – life, to be honest. So I called my broker. He wasn't in. Dropped into my club. Full of old colonial buffers. Had a scotch and soda, picked up an evening paper, put it back. Full of elections and wars and rumours of wars. And I thought – who the bloody hell cares frankly? What does it all matter? What happens to anyone? What happens to me? No-one'd miss me. I wouldn't miss me. I could quite easily just –

(He takes a slug of scotch. Knocks it back.)

And then I thought – wait a minute! Come on Hannay! Pull yourself together man!

Find something to do, you bloody fool! Something mindless and trivial. Something utterly pointless. Something –

(He has a brainwave.)

– I know! A West End show![1] That should do the trick!

(He marches out.)

(Music: Mr. Memory Theme)

(Footlights come up)

---

1. If performing outside London, you could try 'I know! A visit to the theatre!' Or 'A trip to London's popular West End!'

Scene Two: Cockney Music Hall. London.

(Two men appear. We can call these the two **CLOWNS**. *They play a* **COMPERE** *and* **MR MEMORY**. *They are in evening dress and dicky bows. Both have toothbrush moustaches.)*

COMPERE. Thank you ladies and gentlemen. And now with your kind attention I have the immense honour and privilege to presentin' to you one of the most remarkable men ever in the whole world. Mr Memory!!!

(canned applause)

*(***MR MEMORY*** bows.)*

Every day Mr Memory commits to memory fifty new facts and remembers every one of them! Facts from history and from geography, from newspapers and scientific books. In fact, more facts is in his brain than is possible to conceive!

(canned applause)

*(***HANNAY*** appears in a theatre box. Puffs at his pipe. He applauds with the audience.)*

Settle down now please. I will also mention that before retirin' Mr Memory has kindly consented to leaving his entire brain to the British Museum for scientific purposes. Thank you.

*(***MEMORY*** bows.)*

(canned applause)

MEMORY. Thankoo. I will now place myself in a state of mental readiness for this evenin's performance and clear my inner bein' of all exentrinsic and supernumary material.

(drum roll)

(A woman appears next to **HANNAY**. *She is beautiful and nervous in a plunging black 1930s evening gown. Her name is* **ANNABELLA SCHMIDT**.)*

ANNABELLA. Is this seat taken?

HANNAY. Not as far as I know.

*(She sits. Takes out her program. Steals a glance at the audience. **HANNAY** is entranced.)*

(Drum roll stops.)

COMPERE. Now then are you ready for the questions Mr. Memory?

MR MEMORY. Quite ready for the questions, thankoo.

COMPERE. Thankoo.

MR MEMORY. Thankoo.

COMPERE. Now then ladies and gents. First question please. Come on now please –

(Looks round the audience. Points at someone.)

Pardon, sir? What was that, sir? Who won the Cup in 1926?

*(to **MR MEMORY**)*

Who won the Cup in 1926?

MR MEMORY. Who won the cup in 1926? The Tottenham Hotspurs won the cup in 1926 defeatin' the Arsenal Gunners by Five goals to nil in the presence of His Majesty King George the Fifth. Am I right, sir?

COMPERE. Quite right, Mr. Memory!!

MR MEMORY. Thankoo!

(canned applause)

COMPERE. Thankoo. Next question please!

(Looks round the audience. Finds someone else.)

What was Napoleon's horse called?

*(to **MR MEMORY**)*

What was Napoleon's horse called?

MR MEMORY. What was Napoleon's horse called? Napoleon's horse was called Belerophon, what he rode for the final time at Waterlooo, June 15th eighteen-fifteen! Am I right, sir?

COMPERE. Quite right, Mr Memory!!

MR MEMORY. Thankoo.

(canned applause)

COMPERE. Thankoo.

(points at new member of audience)

What was that sir? How old's Mae West? How old's Mae West, Mr. Memory?

MR MEMORY. Well, I know sir – but I never tell a lady's age!

(He finds this very amusing.)

(canned laughter)

COMPERE. Very good, Mr. Memory!

MR MEMORY. Thankoo.

COMPERE. Thankoo. Now then – a serious question please.

*(**HANNAY** stands.)*

HANNAY. I say!

COMPERE. Who was that? Yes, sir?

*(**ANNABELLA** looks panicked. Hides behind her program.)*

HANNAY. How far is Winnipeg from Montreal?

MR MEMORY. Ah! A gentleman from Canada! You're welcome sir!

*(Audience applause. **HANNAY** waves. **ANNABELLA** hides.)*

HANNAY. Thank you.

COMPERE. How far is Winnipeg from Montreal, Mr. Memory?

MR MEMORY. Winnipeg from Montreal sir? Winnipeg from Montreal? One thousand four hundred and fifty four miles. Am I right sir?

HANNAY. Quite right.

MR MEMORY. Thankoo sir!!!

COMPERE. Thankoo sir!

(canned applause)

(ANNABELLA peers into audience. Sees what she's been dreading. Recoils.)

ANNABELLA. Sheisse!

HANNAY. Are you alright?

ANNABELLA. Thank you, yes.

COMPERE. And the next question please!

(ANNABELLA pulls a gun out of her handbag. Shoots into the air. Dust falls from the flies. She hides it quickly.)

(Canned audience pandemonium.)

HANNAY. *(to ANNABELLA)* Did you hear that?

COMPERE. Calm down, Ladies and Gents! Calm down PLEASE!

ANNABELLA. Excuse me?

HANNAY. Yes?

ANNABELLA. May I come home with you?

HANNAY. What's the big idea?

ANNABELLA. Well – I'd like to.

COMPERE. Calm down PLEASE!!!!

HANNAY. Well, it's rather tricky at the moment. You see, I've got the decorators in and –

ANNABELLA. *PLEASE! You have to!*

HANNAY. Well, it's your funeral!

(She runs from her seat. He follows her. They exit.)

(MR MEMORY hasn't got over the gunshot. He is in shock. He runs up and down the stage.)

MR MEMORY. What was Napoleon's horse called? Winnipeg. What defeated King George the Fifth by Five goals to nil. Am I right, sir?

(COMPERE catches him.)

COMPERE. Very good, Mr. Memory.

MR MEMORY. Next question please!

COMPERE. That's enough Mr. M!

MR MEMORY. Beg pardon sir?

COMPERE. *(into the pit)* Play man, play!!

MR MEMORY. I know sir but I never tell a lady's –

(Mr. Memory music.)

COMPERE. That was Mr. Memory!

MR MEMORY. Thankoo!!

COMPERE. Don't forget his name now!

MR MEMORY. Thankoo! Thankoo!

COMPERE. Mr. Memory!

MR MEMORY. Thankoo!

COMPERE. Thankoo!

(The **COMPERE** *pushes him off.)*

(Music and applause cuts out.)

(Lights change.)

Scene Three: Hannay's Flat. Night.

(We hear **HANNAY**'s *voice in the dark.)*

HANNAY. Never can find the switch. Dammit!

*(***HANNAY*** pulls the switch on the standard lamp.)*

(Lights up on **HANNAY**'s *armchair and table. Various ladders, sheets, paint pots revealed.)*

ANNABELLA. Turn it off! Quickly!

*(***HANNAY*** turns off the light. Now the room is illuminated by street lighting coming through the window. Maybe a flashing neon hotel sign. She runs to the window. Looks out.)*

ANNABELLA. Sheisse! *(looks at* **HANNAY***)* Bleint!

HANNAY. Sorry?

ANNABELLA. Bleint!

HANNAY. Bleint?

ANNABELLA. *Bleint! Bleint! Pull the bleint!!*

HANNAY. Oh blind! Of course. Sorry. Blind. Yes.

(Pulls blind down. It snaps back. Pulls it down again. It snaps back. Pulls it down harder. It stays. He walks away. The blind snaps back. He pulls it, wrestles with it, jams it ferociously.)

HANNAY. Sorry about that.

ANNABELLA. Now the light Mr. Hannay!

HANNAY. Light. Right.

(He switches on the light. She marches to the drinks cabinet. Pours herself a drink. Downs it in one.)

Have a drink why don't you?

ANNABELLA. Thank you.

(Pours herself another. Downs it.)

For you?

HANNAY. Thank you.

*(***ANNABELLA*** pours another. Downs this one too.)*

ANNABELLA. Mr. Hannay –

HANNAY. How do you know my name?

ANNABELLA. I saw it in the lobby.

HANNAY. Ah, yes.

(Telephone rings.)

HANNAY. Hello. There's the telephone.

ANNABELLA. Don't answer it, please!

HANNAY. Why not?

ANNABELLA. Because I think it is for me.

*(**HANNAY** picks up the phone. It goes on ringing. An awkward moment for the actors.)*

ANNABELLA. Please don't answer!!

*(**HANNAY** drops the phone on its cradle. The ringing continues then stops.)*

HANNAY. Now look here –

ANNABELLA. Yes?

HANNAY. Am I allowed to know your name?

ANNABELLA. You don't want to know my name.

HANNAY. Don't I?

ANNABELLA. Schmidt.

HANNAY. Schmidt?

ANNABELLA. Annabella Schmidt.

HANNAY. So what's the story Annabella Schmidt?

ANNABELLA. Mr. Hannay?

HANNAY. Yes?

ANNABELLA. May I be very impertinent for a moment and ask for something to eat?

HANNAY. But of course. Would you care for some haddock?

ANNABELLA. Haddock would be wunderbar thank you.

HANNAY. Nothing like a spot of haddock. Now look here –

ANNABELLA. Yes?

HANNAY. It was you who fired that revolver in the theatre, wasn't it? It wasn't a great show but it wasn't that bad.

ANNABELLA. It was a diversion. There were two men in the theatre trying to shoot me.

HANNAY. You should be more careful in choosing your gentlemen friends.

ANNABELLA. No jokes Mr. Hannay, please!

HANNAY. Beautiful mysterious woman pursued by gunmen. Sounds like a spy story.

ANNABELLA. That's exactly what it is. Only I prefer the word 'agent' better.

HANNAY. 'Secret agent' I suppose? For which country?

ANNABELLA. I have no country.

HANNAY. Born in a balloon, eh?

ANNABELLA. Mr. Hannay please! I am being pursued by a very brilliant secret agent of a certain foreign power who is on the point of obtaining highly confidential information VITAL to your air defence. I tracked two of his men to that Music Hall. Unfortunately they recognised me.

HANNAY. Ever heard of a thing called persecution mania?

ANNABELLA. You don't believe me?

HANNAY. Frankly, I don't.

ANNABELLA. They are in the street this moment. Beneath your English lamp-post. Take a look why don't you? *But be careful!*

(**HANNAY** *peers through the blind. The two clowns appear. They wear sinister trilbies under the single glare of a street light.* **HANNAY** *turns back.*)

ANNABELLA. Now do you believe me?

(**HANNAY** *peers through the blind again. The men are still there.*)

HANNAY. You win.

ANNABELLA. Mr. Hannay, I'm going to tell you something which is not very healthy. It will mean either life. Or death. But if I tell you, then you are – *(She gazes at him.)* – involved!

(*The sound of a 30s police car in the distance.*)

HANNAY. Involved?

ANNABELLA. You wish to be – involved?

*(**HANNAY** marches to the blind again. Peers through. The men are there, but slightly late. **HANNAY** sighs irritably. He turns back to **ANNABELLA**.)*

HANNAY. Tell me!

ANNABELLA. Very well. Have you ever heard of the –

(She lowers her voice.)

– Thirty-Nine Steps?

HANNAY. What's that a pub?

ANNABELLA. Your English humour will not help Mr. Hannay! These men will stick at nothing. And I am the only person who can stop them. If they are not stopped, it is only a matter days, perhaps hours before the top secret and highly confidential information is out of the country. And when they've got it out of the country God help us all!

HANNAY. What about the police?

ANNABELLA. *(laughs harshly)* The police! They would not believe me any more than you did! With their boots and their whistles! It is up to us, Mr. Hannay! I tell you these men act quickly! You don't know how clever their chief is. I know him very well. He has a dozen names! He can look like a hundred people! But one thing he cannot disguise. This part –

(lifts her little finger)

– of his little finger is missing. So if ever you should meet a man with no top joint there –

(She gazes at him.)

– be very careful my friend.

HANNAY. I'll remember that.

(He gazes back.)

ANNABELLA. Mr. Hannay?

HANNAY. Richard.

ANNABELLA. Richard.

HANNAY. Yes?

ANNABELLA. May I stay the night please?

   (electricity between them)

HANNAY. Of course. You can – sleep in my bed.

ANNABELLA. Thank you.

HANNAY. I'll get a shakedown on the armchair.

ANNABELLA. *(raises an eyebrow)* As you wish. And one more thing –

HANNAY. Your haddock?

ANNABELLA. Mein haddock?

   (She laughs.)

   I have rather lost the taste for haddock. No! I need –

HANNAY: Yes?

ANNABELLA. A map of Scotland.

HANNAY. Scotland?

ANNABELLA. There's a man in Scotland who I must visit next if anything is to be done. An Englishman. He lives in a –

   (looks around her)

   – big house

HANNAY. A big house?

ANNABELLA. At a place called Alt-na-shellach.

HANNAY. I beg your pardon?

ANNABELLA. Alt-na-shell-ach!

HANNAY. Alt-na-shell-ach. And the Thirty Nine –

ANNABELLA. Bring it to my room.

HANNAY. Certainly.

ANNABELLA. Good night Richard.

   (Turns seductively away, disappears into the darkness.
   HANNAY *gazes after her. Confused and mesmerized.*
   Wishing he could go with her.)

HANNAY. Goodnight Annabella!

Scene Four: Hannay's Flat. Very Late.

(Midnight atmos. Wind. A ticking clock. A 30s police car far away. A distant train whistles.)

(HANNAY tosses and turns restlessly in his cramped armchair.)

(Suddenly ANNABELLA appears. Her pale face looming out of the darkness.)

(Haunting music plays.)

(She drifts seductively towards him. In her hand she holds a map.)

ANNABELLA. *(husky)* Richard?

HANNAY. Annabella?

ANNABELLA. *(even huskier)* Oh Richard – Richard –

HANNAY. Now look here, Annabella. You just breeze into my life from nowhere – you get me all – you know – *involved* and – well – actually I've never met anyone quite like you and – and frankly to be – quite frank –

(She leans over him, breathing deeply. He gazes up at her. He thinks they're going to kiss. He closes his eyes in readiness. Suddenly she gasps loudly and collapses over him, a gleaming knife sticking in her back. He recoils in horror. Turns her over.)

ANNABELLA. Oh Richard! Richard!

(She gazes up at him tenderly.)

I am so sorry. So very sorry.

(She clutches his hand.)

Richard!

HANNAY. Yes?

ANNABELLA. These men. They act quickly! They will stop at nothing. Nothing! You hear me? Now there is –

(barely audible)

– no turning back! Oh, my dear Richard!

(Her eyes widen. Winces in pain.)

ANNABELLA. *(cont.) Alt-na-shellach!!!*

(Her body goes into last paroxysms. She lies dead in his arms.)

HANNAY. Golly!

(He closes her eyes. Struggles awkwardly from beneath her. He sees the map. Pulls it from her already stiff hand. Starts to open it fold by fold. The map is enormous. It goes on opening. He wrestles with it. Battles with it. Searches for what he is looking for. At last he finds it.)

Alt-na-Shellach!

(He looks up.)

Alt-na-Shellach!

(The phone rings.)

(tense music)

(HANNAY spins round. He marches over to the phone. Is about to pick up. Suddenly ANNABELLA's warning words echo in his head.)

ANNABELLA. There is a man in Scotland…only a matter of days!

(HANNAY's hand freezes over the ringing phone.)

Perhaps hours…before the secret is out of the country…

I tell you these men…will stop at nothing…they act quickly! Quickly! Quickly! Quickly!

(The phone rings get louder and louder, chiming in with ANNABELLA's 'Quicklys'.)

(The phone stops ringing.)

(HANNAY thinks fast. He grabs a dust-sheet, covers the body, pockets the enormous map and stands alone, eyes darting.)

(blackout)

(bird-song)

Scene Five: Lobby. Morning

(On comes the **MILKMAN** *whistling the* **MR MEMORY** *theme.* **HANNAY** *bursts out of his front door. They collide.)*

MILKMAN. Blimey mate. Whatchoo up to? I nearly died a' fright.

HANNAY. Could you use a pound note brother?

MILKMAN. A pound note? A pound note? What's the catch?

HANNAY. I need your cap and coat.

MILKMAN. Cap and coat? Cap and coat? What's the game! Spit it out!

HANNAY. I need to make a get-away.

MILKMAN. Do a bunk?

HANNAY. Yes.

MILKMAN. Whatchoo bin up to?

HANNAY. I'm going to have to trust you. There's been a murder committed on the first floor.

MILKMAN. A murder? A murder? By who? By you?

HANNAY. No, no. *(He points.)* By those two men over there.

MILKMAN. I see. So now they're waiting good as gold for a copper to come and arrest 'em, eh?

HANNAY. It's quite true I tell you. They're spies, foreigners. They've murdered a woman in my flat and now they're waiting for me.

MILKMAN. Ah come off it! Funny jokes at five o'clock in the morning.

HANNAY. Alright, alright. I'll tell you the truth. Are you married?

MILKMAN. Yes but don't rub it in.

HANNAY. Well I'm not you see, I'm a bachelor.

MILKMAN. Lucky you.

HANNAY. But I've been seeing this married woman.

MILKMAN. Naughty.

HANNAY. Point is –

MILKMAN. Yeah?

HANNAY. She was leading me on.

MILKMAN. No!

HANNAY. It was all a set up.

MILKMAN. Would you believe it!

HANNAY. See those two men over there?

MILKMAN. I do.

HANNAY. You know who they are?

MILKMAN. Don't tell me!

HANNAY. One's her brother. The other's her husband!

MILKMAN. Cor blimey! I wouldn't be in your shoes! 'Ere have my cap and coat.

(takes off his cap and coat)

HANNAY. Thank you.

*(***HANNAY*** puts on the cap and coat.)*

MILKMAN. Perfick!

HANNAY. I say.

(puts his hand in the pocket, gives him a note)

Take a pound.

MILKMAN. A pound! That's very kind of you!

HANNAY. *(gives him another)* Take two!

MILKMAN. Two pounds! God bless yer guv! Leave the pony round the corner. You'll do the same for me one day.

*(***HANNAY*** runs off. Exits. ***MILKMAN*** looks at the money. Looks at us.)*

Hang on! That's outta my coat! That's my money you just give me! Oi! Come back 'ere! Oi!

*(He chases after ***HANNAY***. Exits)*

Scene Six: Hannay's Flat. Morning.

(**MRS HIGGINS** *the charlady enters.*)

MRS HIGGINS. Mornin' Mr. 'annay! 'ow yer keepin'? What a lovely morning this morning it is this morning. What about this 'ere heat wave! Never seen nothing like it. People droppin like –

(*Pulls dust-sheet off* **ANNABELLA**. *Freezes. Screams a blood-curdling silent Munch-like scream.*)

(*Segues into deafening train whistle.*)

(*Train music.*)

Scene Seven: Edinburgh Train. Day.

(**THE COMPANY** *create the railway carriage.*)

(*The two clowns are now garrulous* **UNDERWEAR SALESMEN***. They sway with the train.*)

(*Train sounds. Hoots and whistles.*)

SALESMAN 1. Well for one thing they're much prettier than they were twenty years ago.

SALESMAN 2. More free.

SALESMAN 1. Free and easy.

(*They share a wink. Wink at* **HANNAY***.* **HANNAY** *shrinks under his hat.*)

SALESMAN 2. Remember the old fashioned sort?

SALESMAN 1. All bones and no bends.

SALESMAN 2. My wife!

(*They roar with laughter, wink at* **HANNAY***. Train whistles.*)

Look at this now!

(**SALESMAN 2** *delves into a small samples case and produces a 1940s white lacy suspender belt. They gaze at it in wonder.* **HANNAY** *gazes too.*)

Our new streamlined model number one.

SALESMAN 1. A glory to behold. Anything to go with it?

SALESMAN 2. Look at this little beauty!

(*He delves some more. Produces an exotic white lacy brassiere.* **HANNAY** *and the* **SALESMEN** *gaze mesmerised as it sways before them.*)

SALESMAN 1. Now that's a sight for sore eyes!

SALESMAN 2. You can say that again! The Two Wonders of the Modern World!

SALESMAN 1. Tell you what? Bring 'em back when they're filled.

(*The* **SALESMEN** *explode with laughter. Wink at* **HANNAY***.*)

SALESMAN 2. Get it?

SALESMAN 1. Get it?

SALESMAN 2. When they're filled!

SALESMAN 1. When they're filled!

SALESMAN 2. Don't be shy!

SALESMAN 1. Don't be shy!

*(**HANNAY** manages a chuckle.)*

SALESMAN 2. That's the spirit!

SALESMAN 1. That's the spirit!

SALESMAN 2. Where are we now?

*(**SALESMAN 1** looks out of the window. He rapidly reads three passing signs.)*

SALESMAN 1. Halifax… Durham… Berwick-Upon-Tweed…

(He sits back in his seat, produces a packet of biscuits.)

Biscuit?

SALESMAN 2. Much obliged.

SALESMAN 1. *(to Hannay)* Biscuit?

HANNAY. No, thank you.

SALESMAN 1. Suit yourself.

*(The **SALESMEN** chomp their biscuits in unison. They watch **HANNAY** and grin broadly. Train whistles and stopping noises.)*

SALESMAN 1. Here we are. Edinburgh Town.

SALESMAN 2. That was quick!

(The train halts. They all lurch.)

(Bagpipe Music: "Scotland the Brave")

Scene Eight: Edinburgh Station. Day.

SALESMAN 1. Wonder what won the two o'clock at Windsor.

SALESMAN 2. I'll get a paper.

SALESMAN 1. I'll go to the lavatory.

(They get up. Squeeze round each other.)

SALESMAN 1. Excuse me. Sorry. Sorry.

SALESMAN 2. Sorry. Sorry.

HANNAY. Sorry.

*(**SALESMAN 1** exits. **SALESMAN 2** sticks his head out of the window. Whistles through his teeth. **SALESMAN 1** immediately back on as a **PAPERBOY** in a flat cap.)*

PAPERBOY. Evenin paper! Latest news! Evenin paper! Latest –

SALESMAN 2. Evenin paper please?

PAPERBOY. Evening paper sir? Thankoo sir!

(gives him a paper)

SALESMAN 2. *(gives him a penny)* Thankoo.

PAPERBOY. Evenin paper! Latest news! Evenin paper! Latest –

*(Exits. Immediately back on as **SALESMAN 1**)*

SALESMAN 1. Excuse me. *(Squeezes past.)* Sorry. Sorry.

SALESMAN 2. Sorry. Sorry.

HANNAY. Sorry.

*(**SALESMAN 1** sits down. He greets **SALESMAN 2**.)*

SALESMAN 2. Hello!

SALESMAN 1. Hello!

SALESMAN 2. *(opens paper)* Good Lord!

SALESMAN 1. What is it?

SALESMAN 2. Been a woman murdered in a fashionable West End flat!

*(**HANNAY** freezes.)*

SALESMAN 1. All these sex dramas. Don't appeal to me! What won?

SALESMAN 2. What won what?

SALESMAN 1. The two O'clock at Windsor.

SALESMAN 2. Two O'clock at Windsor?

*(Turns paper over. They read the back. **HANNAY** peers at the front.)*

Bachelor Boy.

SALESMAN 1. Good.

SALESMAN 2. At seven-to-four on.

SALESMAN 1. Not so good.

*(**SALESMAN 2** back to front page. **HANNAY** sits back quickly.)*

SALESMAN 2. Anyway where was we? Ah yes. *(reads)* Stabbed in the back she was. Portland Mansions. Portland Place.

SALESMAN 1. By the BBC? That's the place to put someone to sleep!

*(They laugh uproariously. Wink at **HANNAY**.)*

What was she like? One of the usual?

SALESMAN 2. *(reads)* Well-dressed woman about thirty-five. *(looks up)* Terrible!

SALESMAN 1. Terrible!

*(They look at **HANNAY**.)*

HANNAY. Terrible!

SALESMAN 2. *(reads)* The tenant Richard Hannay is missing.

SALESMAN 1. You do surprise me!

SALESMAN 2. Approximately thirty-seven. Dark wavy hair. Piercing blue eyes. Pencil moustache.

*(**HANNAY** hides his moustache with his hat.)*

HANNAY. Excuse me?

SALESMEN. Yes?

HANNAY. Might I have a look at your paper?

SALESMAN 1. Certainly.

HANNAY. Thank you.

> (**HANNAY** *takes the paper. Pores into it. Looks up to see both men staring at him. They grin unnervingly.*)

SALESMAN 2. Think I'll pop out to the buffet car. Finished?

> (*snatches paper from* **HANNAY**)

Fancy anythin'?

SALESMAN 1. No thank you.

HANNAY. No thank you.

SALESMAN 2. Right you are.

> (*He leaves the compartment. Squeezes past.*)

SALESMAN 2. Excuse me. Sorry. Sorry.

SALESMAN 1. Sorry. Sorry.

HANNAY. Sorry.

> (**SALESMAN 1** *glances out of the window.*)

SALESMAN 1. Good Heavens! Place is stiff with police!

> (**HANNAY** *freezes.* **SALESMAN 1** *pulls down window. Calls out.*)

Excuse me Constable! Caught the West End murderer yet?

> (**SALESMAN 2** *appears in a police hat.*)

POLICEMAN. We'll catch him, don't you worry sir!

SALESMAN 1. That's the spirit!

> (**POLICEMAN** *changes into porter's hat.*)

PORTER. All aboard for the Highlands! Next stop the highlands!

> (*Changes into PC hat.*)

POLICEMAN. Anything suspicious let us know sir!

SALESMAN 1. Oh yes. Don't you worry!

> (*PC changes into porter's hat.*)

PORTER. All aboard! All aboard!

(**SALESMAN 1** *puts on paperboy hat.*)

PAPERBOY. Final edition sir? Final edition.

(**PORTER** *changes into* **SALESMAN 2** *hat.*)

SALESMAN 2. No thank you!

(**SALESMAN 2** *puts on porter hat.*)

PORTER. All aboard! All aboard!

(**PAPERBOY** *puts on salesman hat.*)

SALESMAN 1. Alright, alright!

(**PORTER** *puts on policeman hat.*)

POLICEMAN. Keep your eyes peeled won't you sir!

SALESMAN 1. Certainly will constable!

POLICEMAN. Don't forget sir!

SALESMAN 1. No I won't constable.

(changes into paperboy hat)

PAPERBOY. Read all about it!! Read all about it!!

(**POLICEMAN** *puts on porter hat.*)

PORTER. All aboard! All aboard!

(**PORTER** *puts on police hat.*)

POLICEMAN. Anything suspicious, let us know sir.

(**PAPERBOY** *changes into* **SALESMAN 1.**)

SALESMAN 1. Will do, constable.

(**POLICEMAN** *puts on porter hat.*)

PORTER. All aboard! All aboard!

(**SALESMAN 1** *changes into* **MRS HIGGINS** *hat.*)

MRS HIGGINS. Is this the 9.41 to Reading?

PORTER. Platform Twelve!

MRS HIGGINS. Thankoo!

PORTER. All aboard let's be havin' yer!

(blows whistle)

(**MRS HIGGINS** *puts on paperboy hat.*)

PAPERBOY. Read all about it!! Read all about it!!

PORTER. All aboard! All aboard!

(blows whistle)

PAPERBOY. Final Edition! Final Edition!

PORTER. All aboard! All ab –

(blows whistle)

(**HANNAY** *the actor can't take any more.*)

HANNAY. Oh just get on with it!!

BOTH CLOWNS. Thankoo!

(Clowns run off. Train shrieks. Chugs out of the station.)

Scene Nine: Highland Train. Day

(The **CLOWNS** *return to their seats. Squeeze past each other. Squeeze past* **HANNAY***.)*

SALESMAN 2. Excuse me. Sorry. Sorry.

SALESMAN 1. Sorry. Sorry.

HANNAY. Sorry.

SALESMAN 2. Well, back from the buffet! Listen to this!

SALESMAN 1. What?

SALESMAN 2. The police are searching the train!

*(***HANNAY** *freezes.)*

Every compartment!

SALESMAN 1. *Every compartment!?*

SALESMAN 2. Listen here's a corker. There was a young man from Nantucket –

HANNAY. Excuse me!

(He leaps up. Slides open the door of the compartment.)

SALESMAN 1. Hope you don't mind us talking shop?

HANNAY. No, no, not at all no.

SALESMAN 1. We're on the run you see.

SALESMAN 2. From our wives!

SALESMAN 1. Never go home!

SALESMAN 2. We ride the railways and sell underwear!

SALESMAN 1. That's all we do!

(They roar with laughter.)

SALESMAN 2. A young man from Nantucket, grew a Venus Fly-trap in a bucket, he said when it grew, now what do I do, do I keep it for breeding or –

(Train shrieks. **HANNAY** *escapes down the corridor.)*

HANNAY. *Sorry!*

SALESMAN 2. He's in a rush!

(They whoosh into a tunnel. Heightened train noises. Stage lights flicker.)

*(***HANNAY** *races along the corridor in the flickering lights.)*

(**SALESMAN 1** *becomes* **POLICEMAN 1**. *Looking into imaginary compartments.*)

POLICEMAN 1. Excuse me please. Sorry to disturb ye. Have ye seen this man? His name is Richard Hannay.

(**HANNAY** *freezes. About turns. Freezes again.*)

(*Now* **SALESMAN 2** *is* **POLICEMAN 2**. *Approaching from the opposite direction. Looking into imaginary compartments.*)

POLICEMAN 2. Excuse me please. Sorry to disturb ye. Have ye seen this man? His name is Richard Hannay.

(**HANNAY** *is trapped. Both policemen march towards him.*)

(*Simultaneously a magical blue light comes up on* **PAMELA** *who appears before him in another compartment.*)

(*She removes her glasses and lets her book fall on to her lap. She runs a hand through her hair and gazes out of the window. She is breathtakingly beautiful, wears a small black top and thigh-hugging pencil skirt.* **HANNAY** *gazes at her, entranced.*)

(*The two* **POLICEMEN** *get closer and closer.* **HANNAY** *looks at the* **POLICEMEN**, *looks into* **PAMELA**'s *compartment. He bursts in. Sweeps her into his arms.*)

HANNAY. Darling! How lovely to see you!

(*He kisses her passionately. She is too shocked to gasp.*)

(*Romantic music.*)

(*The two* **POLICEMAN** *meet at the door. Stare wide-eyed as* **HANNAY** *and* **PAMELA** *kiss.*)

POLICEMAN 1. Someone having a free lunch in there!

POLICEMAN 2. And a free pudding, too, I wouldn't wonder.

(*They titter and exit.*)

(**HANNAY** *pulls back at last.* **PAMELA** *stares at him aghast.*)

(*Romantic music cuts out.*)

HANNAY. Listen I'm so terribly sorry! But I was desperate! I had to do it! My name's Richard Hannay. They're

after me for murder. I swear I'm innocent! You've got
to help me! I've got to keep free for the next few days.
You see the safety of this country depends upon it –

(The two **POLICEMEN** *appear again at the compartment
door.)*

POLICEMAN 1. So sorry to disturb ye but have either of ye
seen a man passing in the last few minutes? His name
is Richard Hannay.

(PAMELA *stares at* **HANNAY.** *All wait while she decides.)*

PAMELA. This is the man you want Inspector!

POLICEMAN 1. But we came by just noo and saw you both –
well you know…

PAMELA. He pushed in here and forced himself upon me.
His name is Richard Hannay!

POLICEMAN 2. Is your name Richard Hannay?

HANNAY. Certainly not.

POLICEMAN 2. But this attractive young lady clearly stated –

(HANNAY *pushes open the door. Leaps out of the train.*
PAMELA *screams. Deafening whooshing train sounds
and wind effects.)*

POLICEMAN 2. After him constable!

POLICEMAN 1. Right sir.

(POLICEMAN 1 *leaps after* **HANNAY** *who is inching
along the outside of the train, hanging onto his hat.*
POLICEMAN 1 *looks down and GASPS!)*

We're on the Forth Bridge sir!!!

POLICEMAN 2. *(from the window)* I can see that constable!
Grab him man!

POLICEMAN 1. Very good sir.

(PC 1 *lunges for* **HANNAY** *and grabs him.* **PC 2** *reaches
from the window. Grabs* **PC 1.** **HANNAY** *leaps to the next
carriage. Pulls* **PC 1** *after him, pulling* **PC 2** *half out of
the rushing train.)*

PAMELA. Can I help?

POLICEMAN 2. *(hanging out of the train, through the rushing wind)* Not right now, miss.

PAMELA. I'll stand here then.

POLICEMAN 2. Very good miss.

> *(The train roars into a tunnel. Lights flicker and flash.* **POLICEMAN 1** *battles with* **HANNAY** *clinging to the train.* **HANNAY** *pulls one way,* **POLICEMAN 1** *pulls the other. Pulling* **POLICEMAN 2** *further and further out of the window.)*[2]

PAMELA. Just a thought?

POLICEMAN 2. *(hanging out of the train)* Yes, miss?

PAMELA. What about the communication cord?

POLICEMAN 2. Good idea, miss.

PAMELA. Shall I pull it?

POLICEMAN 2. Best if I do, miss.

PAMELA. Rightho.

> **(POLICEMAN 2** *reaches painfully back for the communication cord. This pulls* **POLICEMAN 1** *and* **HANNAY** *back again.* **POLICEMAN 2**'s *arm alarmingly elongates.* **PAMELA** *watches wide-eyed. At last* **POLICEMAN 2** *reaches the cord. He grabs the cord.)*

POLICEMAN 2. Pulling the communication cord NOW!

POLICEMAN 1. *(shrieks)* No sir! Not the communication –

> **(POLICEMAN 2** *pulls the cord. The brakes slam on. The train lurches.* **POLICEMAN 1** *loses his grip on* **HANNAY** *who flies away. The* **POLICEMEN** *crash back into* **PAMELA** *who screams as the train screeches to a juddering halt.)*

> *(blackout)*

> *(Music: Ethereal, mystic choirs)*

> *(Lights come up on the familiar structure of the Forth Bridge. Magically created from the three decorators ladders perhaps. It looks magnificent and awesome in the blue light and mist.)*

---

2. The train chase should be open to ingenuity and resources available. I like the idea of the chase down the side of the train, as in the splendid West End and Broadway poster. Or they could go along the top. Or even underneath – Indiana Jones style. The text should fit most scenarios.

Scene Ten: Forth Bridge. Night.

*(Wind sounds. The creaking of girders. Distant fog-horns. **HANNAY** appears out of the mist. He is hanging perilously on the bridge. Miles above the water. He inches his way, gripping on to the cold steel girders.)*

*(The two **PC**s appear. Edging towards him. They get closer and closer. **HANNAY** looks at them. Looks down. Looks at his slipping fingers. Looks at us.)*

HANNAY. *OH CRIKEY!*

(He plunges into the darkness. A long whistle. A tiny splash.)

*(The two **POLICEMEN** look down. Look at each other.)*

(blackout)

(Sound: morse code "beeps" fill the theatre.)

RADIO ANNOUNCER. *(plummy BBC V.O.)* …the suspect Richard Hannay managed to jump from a train on to the Forth Bridge just outside Edinburgh. Police pursued him on to the bridge but he gave them the slip hanging from girders with his bare hands.

Scene Eleven: On the Moors.

(**HANNAY** *appears running across the moors.*)

RADIO ANNOUNCER. *(plummy BBC V.O.)* ...The suspect is approximately thirty-seven and about six foot one. Although he is clearly dangerous, he is quite good looking actually with dark wavy hair, piercing blue eyes and a very attractive pencil moustache. It is not known whether he survived his ordeal. Police had to call off the search in the gathering darkness...

(**HANNAY** *runs out. Swirling mist. Mournful highland wind.*)

Scene Twelve : Crofter's Cottage. Outside.

(**CLOWN 1** *appears. He is* **JOHN McTYTE** *an ancient and surly Scottish crofter. He peers into the mist.* **HANNAY** *appears. The crofter twitches with suspicion.*)

HANNAY. Hello there.

CROFTER. Can I help ye?

HANNAY. Yes I'm um looking for work.

CROFTER. What kind of work?

HANNAY. I'm an itinerant labourer.

CROFTER. Ye'll find nothing in this vicinity.

HANNAY. Are there no –

(significantly)

– big houses round here?

CROFTER. No big houses.

HANNAY. So what's that big house?

CROFTER. What big house?

HANNAY. *(points)* That big house?

CROFTER. Oh that big house.

HANNAY. Isn't that a big house?

CROFTER. That is a big house.

HANNAY. So whose…hoose is that then?

CROFTER. A professor I believe. Professor Jordan. *(twitching)* An Englishman.

HANNAY. An Englishman? It wouldn't be called –

(He takes out the enormous and unruly map. It is even bigger than before. He battles with it.)

– Alt na Shellach, would it?

CROFTER. It would.

HANNAY. Right! Well – thanks very much. I'll try there. Cheerio.

CROFTER. Ye won't tonight!

HANNAY. Won't I?

CROFTER. It's fourteen miles. The other side of the loch.

HANNAY. No really! I'm sure I'll be –

CROFTER. Margaret!

(**MARGARET** *appears. An incredibly pretty Scottish girl.*)

MARGARET. Ay?

CROFTER. Come here! We have a visitor.

(**MARGARET** *crosses to them, head lowered. She looks at* **HANNAY**. *Blushes.*)

MARGARET. Good evening, sir.

(**HANNAY** *sees how incredibly pretty she is. He smiles handsomely.*)

HANNAY. Good evening.

(**MARGARET** *blushes even more.*)

CROFTER. You could stay here if you wanted.

HANNAY. Well on second thoughts that'd be very kind.

CROFTER. Can you eat the herring?

HANNAY. I could murder half a dozen right now.

CROFTER. Can you sleep in a box bed?

HANNAY. I can try.

CROFTER. Two and six.

HANNAY. Done.

CROFTER. See to the gentleman and be quick about it.

HANNAY. Your daughter?

CROFTER. My wife!

HANNAY. Well done.

(**MARGARET** *and* **HANNAY** *look at each other. They look away.*)

CROFTER. Prepare the herring.

MARGARET. Ay.

CROFTER. I'll see to the coos.

HANNAY. Sorry?

CROFTER. I'll see to the coos!

HANNAY. *(still doesn't understand)* Right.

(*The* **CROFTER** *stomps off.*)

MARGARET. Will ye come in?

HANNAY. I'd love to.

Scene Thirteen: Crofter's Cottage.

(HANNAY looks around the miserable cottage. The moaning wind rattles the windows. MARGARET is overwhelmed with shyness. She points to the armchair.)

MARGARET. There's your bed.

(HANNAY looks at the armchair.)

HANNAY. Marvellous.

MARGARET. Could ye sleep there d'ye think?

HANNAY. I could sleep anywhere right now.

(MARGARET blushes.)

MARGARET. Won't you sit down please whilst I go on with our supper?

HANNAY. Thank you.

(He sits down. She busies herself with supper.)

I say?

MARGARET. Yes?

HANNAY. You wouldn't have today's paper?

MARGARET. My husband has the paper.

HANNAY. Right.

(MARGARET shyly lays the table. He watches her.)

So erm – been in these parts long?

MARGARET. No. I'm from Glasgow.

HANNAY. Glasgow?

MARGARET. D'ye ever see it?

HANNAY. No I never did.

MARGARET. Oh ye should. Ye should see Sauchiehall Street on a Saturday night with all its fine shops and the trams and the lights. And the cinema palaces and the crowds.

(a faraway look)

It's Saturday night tonight.

HANNAY. Well I've never been to Glasgow but I've been to Edinburgh and Montreal. And London.

MARGARET. London!

HANNAY. I could tell you all about London at supper.

MARGARET. *(suddenly entranced)* Could ye?

HANNAY. Certainly could.

MARGARET. *(face clouds)* No. John would nae approve o' that I doubt!

HANNAY. John?

MARGARET. My husband. He says it's best not to think of such places and all the wickedness that goes on there.

HANNAY. Or – I could tell you now.

MARGARET. Now?

(He gazes at her.)

HANNAY. If you wanted.

MARGARET. Aye.

(She gazes back.)

Ye could.

(Romantic music)

HANNAY. What would you like to know?

MARGARET. Is it true that all the ladies paint their toe-nails?

HANNAY. Some of them.

MARGARET. And put rouge and lipsticks on their faces?

HANNAY. They do yes.

MARGARET. Do London ladies look beautiful?

HANNAY. They wouldn't if you were beside them.

*(**MARGARET** catches her breath. Turns to him. Their eyes meet. A moment of stunned sexual longing.)*

MARGARET. You ought not to say that.

*(The **CROFTER** bursts in. He carries an evening newspaper.)*

CROFTER. *Ought not to say WHAT!?*

(Romantic music cuts out.)

*(**HANNAY** and **MARGARET** spring away.)*

HANNAY. Oh I was – er – just saying to your wife that I prefer living in the town to the country.

CROFTER. God made the country.

HANNAY. Certainly did!

CROFTER. Supper ready woman?

MARGARET. Almost.

CROFTER. Then hurry yeself!

(*The* **CROFTER** *throws the paper on the table. There is* **HANNAY'S** *photo on the front.* **HANNAY** *freezes.*)

HANNAY. Do you mind if I look at your paper?

CROFTER. Suit yourself.

HANNAY. Thank you.

(**HANNAY** *picks up the paper. Hides the photo. Reads the story as nonchalantly as possible. The* **CROFTER** *watches him suspiciously.*)

CROFTER. Ye did nae tell me your name.

HANNAY. Oh – um – Hammond.

CROFTER. Mr O' Hum Hammond.

HANNAY. No. Hammond!

MARGARET. Here we are.

(*She produces three herrings.*)

HANNAY. Splendid!

CROFTER. I'll say a blessing afore we begin.

HANNAY. Good idea!

(*They all sit round the table. Close their eyes.*)

CROFTER. Oh most mighty and unforgiving father. Sanctify these bounteous and undeserved mercies to us miserable sinners. Make us bow on bended knee, make us truly thankful for all –

(**HANNAY** *opens his eyes. Tries to read the paper again.* **MARGARET** *opens her eyes. Notices him reading.*)

– thy manifold blessings.

(**HANNAY** *notices her noticing him. Now she peeks at the paper. Sees the photo. Realises who he is. Her eyes flash with panic.*)

CROFTER. *(cont.)* And continually turn our loathsome hearts from wickedness –

*(***HANNAY*** *looks back at her. Reassuring her with his eyes.)*

(The **CROFTER** *opens his eyes and sees them gazing earnestly at each other. He twitches madly and finishes grace.)*

– beat our gluttonous thoughts and lash our lustful desires, as with a three-forked flailing stick, pressing our bestial noses to the grindstone and blinding our eyes to the tawdry beads and baubles of all worldly wicked things. Amen.

HANNAY & MARGARET. Amen.

CROFTER. Ach!

(He jumps up.)

I just remembered I forgot to – er – lock the barn. I'll go and – lock it!

MARGARET. Right ye are.

(He goes out, whistling nonchalantly. Almost immediately his mad paranoiac eyes appear through the window. **HANNAY** *and* **MARGARET** *do not notice him. They start miming earnestly and passionately to each other.* **HANNAY** *holds her hands. Begging her to believe him. The* **CROFTER** *watches aghast! His eyes flash and seethe.)*

Scene Fourteen: Crofter's Cottage. Midnight.

(**HANNAY** *asleep in his cramped bed.*)

(*Sound of a car drawing to a halt outside. Headlights flash across the windows.*)

(**MARGARET** *runs in. Looks out of the window. Runs to* **HANNAY**. *Gingerly shakes him.*)

MARGARET. *(whispers)* Wake up, sir! Wake up please, sir!

HANNAY. *(delighted)* Oh hello!

MARGARET. Oh no, sir, no! I don't mean – It's the police, sir, Mr O' Hum Hammond! Wake up I beg of ye, sir!

HANNAY. *(leaps up)* The police!

MARGARET. You must go now while there's still a chance!

(*She grabs his hand. The* **CROFTER** *appears in his nightgown.*)

CROFTER. Ay! I mighta known! Making love behind my back!

(*to* **HANNAY**)

Get oot!

(*to* **MARGARET**)

And as for ye –

(*raises fist*)

HANNAY. *(stepping between them)* Not so fast my friend!

MARGARET. No! Go go! It's your only chance of liberty!

HANNAY. Listen! You're all wrong about this! She's only trying to help me!

CROFTER. Ay! To bring shame and disgrace upon my house!

HANNAY. Actually if you want to know I'm on the run from the police!

CROFTER. *The police!!!*

HANNAY. They're after me for murder!

CROFTER. *Murder!? Police!?*

(Knock knock knock from the door.)

(The **CROFTER** *runs to the door. Peeks through a crack. He runs back.)*

CROFTER. They're right outside!

HANNAY. Don't let them in! Say I'm not here!

(Knock knock knock.)

(The **CROFTER** *is overheating violently.)*

CROFTER. Ach!

(He runs to the door.)

HANNAY. I'll make it worth your while.

*(***CROFTER** *skids to a halt.)*

CROFTER. How much?

HANNAY. Five pounds!

CROFTER. *(eye twitching)* In cash?

HANNAY. Will you take a cheque?

CROFTER. Don't be funny wi' me!

MARGARET. Pay him pay him!

HANNAY. *(takes out a five pound note)* Here!!

(Knock knock knock.)

(The **CROFTER** *grabs the note, runs to the door and slams it behind him.)*

MARGARET. Och, I dinna trust him! Listen!

*(***MARGARET** *runs to the door and listens. We hear muttering outside. She runs back to* **HANNAY.***)*

MARGARET. Ay I was right! He's double crossing ye! Quick! Now's your time! Through the window!

*(***HANNAY** *rushes upstage.)*

MARGARET. Not that window!

HANNAY. Which window?

MARGARET. The rear window! Wait!

HANNAY. What?

MARGARET. Your jacket!

HANNAY. My jacket?

MARGARET. It's terrible light-coloured.

HANNAY. Oh is it? It's the latest Harris Tweed.

MARGARET. I'm afeart they'll see you on the dark moors. Best take this one!

(She gives him a dark overcoat.)

HANNAY. This is your husband's coat!

MARGARET. Ay, his Sunday best. It's so black they'll never see you!

HANNAY. *(brings out a small black book)* What's this?

MARGARET. His hymn book.

HANNAY. I can sing a hymn if I get frightened.

MARGARET. Don't joke I beg of you.

(He holds her. She melts into him.)

HANNAY. What'll happen to you?

MARGARET. Don't worry about me!

(Music builds.)

(They gaze at each other.)

HANNAY. I wish I could take you away from all this!

MARGARET. *(She looks at him yearningly.)* No. This is my home.

HANNAY. What's your name?

MARGARET. Margaret.

HANNAY. Goodbye, Margaret.

(He kisses her)

I'll never forget you for this!

(He kisses her again. More passionately. She surrenders beneath him. Pulls away at last.)

MARGARET. Go now!

*(**HANNAY** escpaes through the window.)*

(Immediately the two policemen rush through the door blowing whistles. They spot him through the window.)

POLICEMAN 1. There he is! After him!

*(The police rush out after **HANNAY**.)*

*(**MARGARET** watches in agony.)*

(The whistles disappear into the distance.)

*(Lights fade on **MARGARET**, her haunted face at the window.)*

(Chase music.)

Scene Fifteen: Scottish Moors. Dawn.

(Lights up on **HANNAY** *on the run. He darts and dodges across the Scottish moors. The policemen appear with dogs on leads. They spot him.* **HANNAY** *runs off. The police and dogs give chase.)*

RADIO ANNOUNCER. *(V.O.)* We are sorry to interrupt this programme of popular Scottish romantic music to set your heart aquiver to bring you an important news-flash. Richard Hannay, wanted in connection with the Portland Place murder has been spotted on the moors near Loch Crimond. Police have warned he is almost certainly armed and dangerous. Here is his description once again. He is approximately thirty-seven and about six foot one. With dark, wavy hair, piercing blue eyes and of course his very attractive pencil moustache. His time on the moors has actually made him slightly more rugged-looking, which makes him look even better looking than he did before.

*(***HANNAY*** *rushes past mid-chase. He happens to hear this. He smiles modestly before running on. The radio continues.)*

The suspect Richard Hannay is currently on foot in inhospitable terrain and police can assure listeners that they are closing in with specialist squads in fugitive apprehension by foot, road and – by air!

*(***HANNAY*** *stops to catch his breath. Looks around. All appears clear. Has he escaped? Suddenly there is a sound in the distance. The ominous buzz of a single-engined Tiger Moth.* **HANNAY** *spins round. Looks up. The sound builds.)*

(A plane appears. The plane gets closer.)

*(***HANNAY*** *starts to run. The plane chases* **HANNAY**.*)*

(Over the P/A we hear the pilots' radio conversation.)

PILOT 1. There he is. Over there!

PILOT 2. Which direction's that then?

PILOT 1. North-by-North West!

PILOT 2. North-by-North West! Why that's the direction of –

PILOT 1. Professor Jordan's house!

PILOT 2. Professor Jordan's house? Why's he going there I wonder?

PILOT 1. No idea!

PILOT 2. He's disappeared again!

PILOT 1. Oh no!

PILOT 2. There he is!

PILOT 1. Shoot man shoot!

(Rattle of machine gun fire. **HANNAY** *ducks and dives. Dodges the bullets. Runs on.)*

(Music builds)

PILOT 2. Missed him! Damn all this impenetrable Scottish mist!

(More machine gun fire. **HANNAY** *dives to the floor again.)*

(The plane whines dangerously.)

PILOT 1. Wait a minute! Oh my God!

PILOT 2. What?

PILOT 1. We're too close to the – *Oh no!*

PILOT 2. *What!!?*

PILOT 1. *Change direction! Change direction!*

PILOT 2. *I can't! I can't!*

PILOT 1. *Oh no! Oh no!*

(Plane nose-dives. Screeches deafeningly.)

PILOT 2. *We're going to –*

PILOT 1. *OH GOD!!!*

PILOTS 1 & 2. *AAAAAAGGGGHHHH!!!!*

(Plane explodes in a spectacular conflagration of smoke and fire.)

(Music climaxes.)

(The stage fills with smoke.)

(A figure appears. It is **HANNAY**. *He is exhausted but still running.)*

(A grand front door appears. And a sign: "ALT NA SHELLACH".)

(He stumbles towards the door. Straightens his tie. Presses the door bell.)

(Avon chimes: Ding dong!)

Scene Sixteen: Alt Na Shellach.

(A severe-looking grey-haired lady in tweeds opens the door **MRS LOUISA JORDAN**. *Played by* **CLOWN** 1.)

MRS JORDAN. Yes?

HANNAY. I am so sorry to disturb you but I'm looking for the professor. Professor Jordan.

MRS JORDAN. Professor Jordan? I am the Professor's wife. Louisa Jordan.

HANNAY. I do beg your pardon Mrs Jordan. May I see the Professor? It's really quite important.

MRS JORDAN. May I know your name?

HANNAY. Yes. My name is Hammond. Tell him a friend of Miss Annabella Schmidt.

MRS JORDAN. Miss Annabella Schmidt? Come in Mr Hammond if you would please.

HANNAY. Thank you.

Scene Seventeen: Alt Na Shellach. Interior.

(She leads him through the baronial corridors. HANNAY looks about him.)

HANNAY. Lovely house.

MRS JORDAN. *(smiling graciously)* We like it.

(They march through several enormous rooms.)

MRS JORDAN. We're just having a few drinks with some friends to celebrate my daughter Hilary's birthday. A number of well-to-do acquaintances of my husband. Including the Sheriff of the County. Later we're organizing a shooting party. Perhaps you'd you care to join us?

HANNAY. Thank you.

MRS JORDAN. Shall we pop into the party?

(She opens the door. Wild shadows dance across their faces.)

(Cocktail Party sound effects/Jitterbug-type music)

(She has second thoughts. Closes the door.)

(Music stops.)

MRS JORDAN. On second thoughts. If you wouldn't mind waiting in here Mr. Hammond. I'll fetch my husband directly.

HANNAY. Certainly.

(She opens the door.)

(Music starts again.)

(Shadows dance. She closes the door behind her.)

(Music stops.)

Scene Eighteen: The Professor's Study.

(**HANNAY** *waits. Looks around. Tentatively opens the door.*)

(*Music starts.*)

(*Shadows dance. He closes the door.*)

(*Music stops.*)

(*tries again*)

(*Music starts.*)

(*Shadows dance. He closes the door.*)

(*Music stops.*)

(*a last tiny look*)

(*Music starts.*)

(*Shadows dance. He closes the door.*)

(*Music stops.*)

(*a voice from behind him:*)

VOICE. Mr. Hammond?

(**HANNAY** *swings round.* **PROFESSOR JORDAN** *is seated in an armchair.*)

PROFESSOR. So sorry to have kept you.

HANNAY. It's quite alright.

PROFESSOR. So you're from Annabella Schmidt?

HANNAY. I am yes.

PROFESSOR. Do you have any news?

HANNAY. She's been murdered!

PROFESSOR. *Murdered!?* Oh dear, yes, of course. The Portland Mansions affair. Quite dreadful. And now the police are after you.

HANNAY. They are rather!

PROFESSOR. Well don't worry about them. I managed to put them off the scent. They'll be far away by now.

HANNAY. Thanks awfully.

PROFESSOR. *(smiling kindly)* Not at all old chap.

HANNAY. I didn't do it!

PROFESSOR. Of course you didn't do it Mr. – Mr. Hannay. I suppose it's safe to call you by your real name now?

HANNAY. Quite safe.

PROFESSOR. Jolly good. But tell me – why did you come all the way to Scotland to tell me about it?

HANNAY. Because I believe she was trying to tell you about some secret top secret air ministry…secret and she was killed by a foreign agent who was interested too.

PROFESSOR. Really? Well I'm so glad you told me! And risking your life into the bargain! How can I ever thank you?

(HANNAY smiles modestly. Then presses on urgently.)

HANNAY. The thing is professor, she was looking for something!

PROFESSOR. Yes?

HANNAY. Something called –

PROFESSOR. Go on.

HANNAY. The Thirty-Nine Steps! If we can find out what the Thirty-Nine Steps are then –

(The professor stands. Still smiling.)

PROFESSOR. So – let me get this quite clear – oh I'm so sorry – you must be exhausted! Do take a seat Mr. Hannay.

(He stands. Proffers him his own armchair. HANNAY sits rather awkwardly. The PROFESSOR smiles.)

PROFESSOR. Better?

HANNAY. Thank you.

PROFESSOR. So did she tell you what this foreign agent looked like?

HANNAY. There wasn't time. Oh! There was one thing. Part of his little finger was missing.

PROFESSOR. Which little finger?

HANNAY. This one I think.

(holds up a little finger)

PROFESSOR. Are you sure it wasn't – this one?

(He holds up his own little finger. It is cut off at the knuckle.)

HANNAY. I'm not sure. I think –

*(The professor pulls out a gun. **HANNAY** gasps!)*

PROFESSOR. Mr. Hannay – I'm afraid I've been guilty of leading you down the garden path. Or should I say – up. I never can remember.

HANNAY. It seems to be the wrong garden alright.

PROFESSOR. Yes. I'm afraid it does. Mr. Hannay, you've forced me into a very difficult position. You see I live here as a respectable citizen. My very best friend is the Sheriff of the County. You must realise my whole existence could be jeopardised if it became known that I was not – how shall I say – not what I seem. You see there's my wife and daughter to think of. But what makes it doubly important that I simply can't let you go is that I'm just about to convey some very vital information out of the country. Oh yes, I've got it alright. I'm afraid poor Annabella would have been far too late. So it seems there is only one option, Mr Hannay.

*(He cocks the gun, aims point blank at **HANNAY**.)*

*(**MRS JORDAN** walks in.)*

(Jitterbug music.)

(She takes in the gun. Doesn't flick an eyelid.)

MRS JORDAN. I shall be serving lunch directly, dear. The Sheriff has to go at three. Will Mr Hammond be staying?

PROFESSOR. I don't think so dear.

*(**MRS JORDAN** smiles and leaves.)*

(Music stops.)

PROFESSOR. Unless of course you decide to join us.

(Lights a cigarette in a black holder.)

HANNAY. For lunch?

PROFESSOR. Very good, Mr. Hannay. You see you're just the kind of man we need. Sharp. Intelligent. Cold-blooded. Ruthless. When the war comes these will be the exact qualities we need.

HANNAY. War?

PROFESSOR. Oh yes! We'll have quite a show of it.

HANNAY. And what if I don't believe in those qualities?

PROFESSOR. What other qualities are there?

HANNAY. Well…human qualities.

PROFESSOR. *Human* qualities! What human qualities?

HANNAY. Loyalty, selflessness, sacrifice…

(pause)

…love…

PROFESSOR. *(He laughs a cruel laugh.)* Love!? Oh please Mr. Hannay! When have you ever *loved* anyone? It's not in your nature, old sport. Never has been, has it? You have no heart, do you Hannay! But you know this.

(HANNAY *sits shocked. How does the professor know his deepest fears?)*

So sad, isn't it? No one to love. No one to care for. No home to go to.

(The professor comes close to **HANNAY,** *pinned in the armchair. Blows smoke into his face.)*

But there is you see. There is – *our home!*

HANNAY. Our home?

PROFESSOR. That is the only place you will find 'love' old chum. Where you really and truly belong.

(We notice a German accent subtly emerging from the professor's cultured British tones. **HANNAY** *stares in horror as the truth starts to dawn.)*

Oh we will give you love, Hannay. And in return? You will love us!! The master race. On our great unstoppable march. Commanded eternally by destiny itself!! Well old sport? What do you say?? Will you join us? Hannay!??

(The **PROFESSOR** *waits excitedly.* **HANNAY** *thinks. The clock ticks in the corner.* **HANNAY** *decides.)*

HANNAY. Alright Professor. If you think I'm suitable material.

PROFESSOR. *(whoops delightedly)* Oh I do! I do, old sport. How unutterably splendid! I will tell Mrs. Jordan.

(He cackles with pleasure. Runs to the door.)

HANNAY. Oh. There's just one thing. Sorry.

PROFESSOR. Of course. Anything!

HANNAY. One little question.

PROFESSOR. Ask away!

HANNAY. Before I sign up.

PROFESSOR. Absolutely mein leibling.

HANNAY. What exactly is erm –

PROFESSOR. Yes yes yes?

HANNAY. – the Thirty-Nine Steps?

PROFESSOR. *The Thirty-Nine Steps!* The Thirty-Nine Steps – though I say it myself – is mein own brilliant idea! The very soul of the enterprise! The very –

(He gasps. Realises **HANNAY***'s ruse.)*

But wait a minute!! Wait a minute! You – you – think you can pull ze vool? Ach!! You thought you could join us and then –

HANNAY. Master race? *I despise you!!!*

(The **PROFESSOR** *staggers back clutching his chest.)*

PROFESSOR. Ach! You are as bad as she was! Anabella Schmidt! With all her outmoded sentimental notions. Her high-minded *DEMOKRATIKISCH BOVEN-SHEISSEDRIVVLE!* I thought for a moment you might – but no! No!! You – you – pathetic – pusilanimous – petty-minded –

(He fires directly at **HANNAY***'s heart.)*

*(***HANNAY** *staggers. Realises he's been shot.)*

HANNAY. Oh bugger.

(He sinks to the floor. The **PROFESSOR** *watches. Cigarette smoke swirling about him.)*

*(***HANNAY** *lies spread-eagled below him.)*

PROFESOR. The Thirty-Nine Steps? I tell you Mr Hannay. *YOU VILL NEVER EVER KNOW!*

(The door flies open. **MRS. JORDAN** *in her tweeds.)*

(Jitterbug music. Very loud and raucous.)

(The **PROFESSOR** *grasps* **MRS JORDAN** *'s hand. They start dancing. They stamp and shout. They become wilder and wilder. A terrible conflagration envelops the stage. The flames lick around the stamping Jordans.)*

*(***HANNAY** *'s body lies motionless.)*

End of Act One

ACT TWO

(Overture)

Scene Nineteen: Sheriff's Office.

*(**CLOWN 2** has his feet up on the table and is laughing loudly. He is the **SHERIFF OF THE COUNTY**. Another man has his back to us.)*

SHERIFF. Cigarette cases. Pocket watches. Spectacle holders. Ha ha ha! But never a hymn book Mr. Hannay!

*(The other man turns. We see it is **RICHARD HANNAY**. Miraculously recovered. And laughing too.)*

Who'd a'thought a hymn book could stop –

(Holds up a silver bullet. Throws it to him.)

– a bullet! Still, I'm not surprised. Some of those hymns are terrible hard to get through.

(They both laugh again.)

And to think I was drinking the villain's champagne only half an hour before!

HANNAY. Right!

SHERIFF. I canna barely believe it. Tea, Mr Hannay?

HANNAY. No thank you.

SHERIFF. Calling himself a professor! Whereas all along he was a –

HANNAY. A spy!

SHERIFF. A spy! Well it's a lesson to us all! Pretty slick sleuthing for an amateur Mr. Hannay!

HANNAY. Thank you.

SHERIFF. Sure about the tea?

HANNAY. Quite sure, thank you! Look here, sheriff, I don't want to rush you or anything but oughtn't we be taking steps? This is serious you know. If it weren't, you don't suppose I'd put myself in your hands with a murder charge hanging over me?

SHERIFF. Ach! Never heed the murder Mr. Hannay! I don't doubt you'll be able to convince Scotland Yard of your innocence as easily as you've convinced me. All I need is a short statement to forward to the proper authority. I've someone coming from the police station next door to take it down. Biscuit?

HANNAY. No biscuit thank you!

SHERIFF. Nice Garibaldi?

HANNAY. Listen, sheriff, there's no time to be lost! He's got the information! And it's absolutely vital to the safety of –

(**CLOWN 1** *bursts through the door as the* **CHIEF INSPECTOR.***)*

INSPECTOR. Are you wishing to see me, sheriff?

SHERIFF. Indeed I am, Chief Inspector! Do you think I enjoy playing for time with a *MURDERER!!!*

HANNAY. *MURDERER???*

CHIEF INSPECTOR. *MURDERER!!!*

SHERIFF. Richard Hannay, you are under arrest! On the charge of wilful murder of a woman unknown in Portland Mansions London on Tuesday last. Take him to the county gaol!

HANNAY. You heard my story! It's true! Every word of it!

SHERIFF. Listen, Hannay! We're not such imbeciles in Scotland as some smart Londoners may think! I don't believe your cock-and-bull story about the professor! Why he's my best friend in the district!

(picks up phone)

Get me Professor Jordan!

HANNAY. If the professor didn't shoot me – where did this bullet come from?

(He holds up the bullet. The **SHERIFF** *and* **INSPECTOR** *recoil cowering.)*

SHERIFF. *Grab him man!*

(The **INSPECTOR** *grabs* **HANNAY**.)

SHERIFF. *(still holding the phone)* Oh ho ho! You're in deep water Hannay and it's getting deeper by the second!

(He hears a voice on the phone. He snaps into the receiver.)

Yes? Who's there? This is the sheriff of the county here and I'll thank you to – Ah! Professor!

(Practically falls to his knees. Bows to the phone.)

I do beg your pardon most humbly, sir. Just to let you know, sir. We have apprehended the villain, sir! Indeedy we have, sir yes sir. Thank you kindly, sir.

HANNAY. I demand that you allow me to speak to the Foreign Office in London.

SHERIFF. *(laughing)* Foreign Office in London! I'm afraid not Mr. Hannay. Handcuffs Inspector, please!

(The **INSPECTOR** *clicks one handcuff on to* **HANNAY**'s *wrist.)*

INSPECTOR. Come along quietly, sir please sir.

SHERIFF. *(on phone)* Handcuffs going on now, sir.

HANNAY. *I don't think so!*

(With an almighty effort, **HANNAY** *pushes the* **INSPECTOR** *into the* **SHERIFF**. *They both crash to the floor.)*

(A window appears. **HANNAY** *does a spectacular leap through it.)*

INSPECTOR. He's escaping!! Stop him!! Stop that man!!

*(***HANNAY** *runs out. The* **INSPECTOR** *follows him blowing his whistle. The* **SHERIFF** *stares at the phone in frozen horror. Puts it to his ear.)*

SHERIFF. No no. Everything's under control, sir. Everything tickety boo, professor. Indeedy indeedy it is, sir.

(Laughs in abject terror. Starts chomping biscuits.)
(police whistles in distance)
(chase music)

Scene Twenty: City Streets

(**HANNAY** *is running through the streets.*)

(*Shadows of policemen appear at every turn. The police shadows give chase.* **HANNAY** *runs madly on. The shadows get taller and taller. Gradually enveloping the whole stage.*)

(*Sound of a marching band. He watches as they pass. He joins in. Escapes.*)

(*Lights up.*)

Scene Twenty-One: Assembly Hall.

(An enormous banner across the back of the stage: "VOTE McCORQUODALE".)

(One of the clowns appears. **MR. DUNWOODY** *Master of Ceremonies. Fussy and doddery, he carries a chair.)*

*(***HANNAY*** *runs on breathlessly.)*

HANNAY. Excuse me! I wonder if you can help me – I'm afraid I'm –

DUNWOODY. With you in a minute!!

HANNAY. Right! Absolutely! Can I help?

DUNWOODY. No thank ye.

HANNAY. The thing is you see –

DUNWOODY. If you don't mind!

HANNAY. Sorry.

*(***MR. D*** *places the chair at the side of the stage.)*

DUNWOODY. There we are now.

HANNAY. Right. Anyway – I'm in a bit of a pickle you see and –

DUNWOODY. *(Looks at* **HANNAY**. *Whoops with delight)* Why! Hello there! Helloo! Helloo!

HANNAY. Hello.

DUNWOODY. You're here at last!

HANNAY. Am I?

DUNWOODY. So good of you to come! We're all here! We're all here! Look! He's here Mr Macquarrie!

(Now the other **CLOWN** *appears. He is the Chairman* **MR MCQUARRIE**. *Even more ancient and doddery. He is dragging on a lectern.)*

MCQUARRIE. Ah! He's here! He's here! Thank the Lord! Thank the lord! Thank the lord!

DUNWOODY. Take a seat take a seat take a seat!

HANNAY. Thank you.

*(The two old men plonk him in the chair, neaten his hair
and straighten his tie.* **HANNAY** *sits. No idea where he is
or what he's doing.)*

*(***DUNWOODY*** *grasps the lectern, beams at the audience.)*

(canned applause)

DUNWOODY. Ladies and Gentlemen, it it now my extreme
pleasure to call upon our ever popular chairman Mr.
McQuarrie to say a few choice words about this evening's illustrious special guest speaker! Mr. McQuarrie
if you would please.

(canned applause)

*(***MCQUARRIE*** *grasps the lectern. Proceeds to address the
audience but entirely inaudibly.)*

MCQUARRIE. Thankee yes…thankee…well Ladies and Gentlemen there's no need for me to tell ye of our special
guest speaker's many and remarkable –

DUNWOODY. Mr McQuarrie, sir.

MCQUARRIE. Ay?

DUNWOODY. Speak up, sir.

MCQUARRIE. Speak up?

DUNWOODY. Speak up. Ay.

MCQUARRIE. Speak up. Ay.

*(Carries on at exactly the same level of inaudibility. The
audience might pick up the odd word but that's all.)*

– special guest speaker's many and remarkable qualities. His brilliant record as soldier, statesman, pioneer
and poet speaks for itself. He is now one of the most
foremost figures in the diplomatic and political world
in the great city of London and the perfect gentleman
to tell ye in no uncertain terms how important it is for
this constituency at this crucial by-election that our
candidate should be returned by an adequate majority.
So without further ado let me call upon our illustrious guest speaker for this evening – Captain Rob Roy
McAlistair!

(wild canned applause)

(The old men nod at **HANNAY** *who sits there smiling. He looks round for Captain McAlistair. Realises they mean him. Looks aghast. Realises there's nothing else for it. Approaches the lectern.)*

HANNAY. Well – ladies and gentlemen I must apologise for my...hesitation in addressing you but to tell you the simple truth, I'd entirely failed, while listening to the chairman's flattering description just now, to realise he was talking...about me.

(canned laughter)

Thank you. Thank you very much. Anyway when I... er...journeyed up to Scotland a few – days ago, travelling on the Highland Express over that magnificent structure the Forth Bridge –

(Reveals his handcuff. Hastily hides it.)

– I'd no idea that in a few days I should be addressing an important political meeting. But may I say from the bottom of my heart and the utmost sincerity how delighted and relieved I am to find myself in your presence at this moment.

(Suddenly **PAMELA** *enters. She waves at* **MCQUARRIE** *and* **DUNWOODY.** **HANNAY** *smiles at her.)*

Oh hello. Do take a seat. I'm just about to get to the best –

(He recognizes her. She recognizes him.)

Good heavens! Hello.

PAMELA. Hello.

(They gaze at one another for a moment. Remembering that kiss. She snaps out of it. Runs out.)

HANNAY. So – anyway, um – what was I saying? Ah yes – delighted. Not to say – relieved. Because so long as I stand on this platform I am delivered for the moment from the cares and anxieties that are always the lot of a man in my position. Anyway ladies and gentlemen as you know we're here tonight to – to – discuss erm

– what shall we discuss? I know – let's discuss er – how about – the herring trade? Or haddock perhaps? Or the idle rich! Not that I can talk about that because I'm not rich and I've never been idle.

(canned laughter)

HANNAY. *(cont.)* Thanks awfully. Well I've been pretty busy all my life really. Well actually not recently. Recently I've been in a bit of a slump to be honest. Catching myself in the lonely hours, full of damned – thoughts and what have you. Well not that recently. Recently, the last few days –

*(**PAMELA** re-appears. Whispers furiously to **MESSRS D &
MCQ**. They leave the stage together. **HANNAY** carries on.
He's rather getting into it.)*

– well the last day really, everything's gone a bit haywire frankly. Wouldn't say it's been easy. Pretty damned difficult actually. But the odd thing is – the odd thing is – you carry on! And it's pretty bracing when you do. Pulls a chap out of himself if you know what I mean. There he is. No idea what's happening. Who to trust. Where to turn. Whether it'll be worth it at the end of it all. But something – I don't know – stirs the old bones!

(He grips the lectern.)

Gets the old ticker pumping again! And there's no time to think. And your mind's singing. And your heart's racing. And you're meeting people. Real people! Doing the best they can! Yes! Doing the best they can in all the terrible situations the world throws at them! Suffering things *no man or woman ought to suffer!* And yet they carry on! They don't give up! They damn well keep going! And I'll tell you what else they do. They do the best they can for *other* people too! Whatever problems they've got, they damn well look after each other! Is that such an –

(He remembers the professor's words.)

– 'outmoded sentimental notion'? Is it!? Well is it? So look here –

(Music: Hubert Parry's "Jerusalem" fades up.)

HANNAY. *(cont.)* – let's just all set ourselves resolutely to make this world a happier place! A decent world! A good world! A world where no nation plots against nation!

*(**PAMELA** appears again. This time accompanied by the two clowns who have now changed into two **HEAVIES** in trilbies and trench-coats. **HANNAY** carries on, playing for time. But inspired too.)*

Where no neighbour plots against neighbour, where there's no persecution or hunting down, where everybody gets a square deal and a sporting chance and where people try to help and not to hinder! A world where suspicion and cruelty and fear have been forever banished! So I'm asking you – each and every one of you here tonight –

(He points at members of the audience.)

– you and you and –

(He searches round.)

– you and you and you and –

(He searches round.)

– definitely you! Is that the sort of world you want? Because that's the sort of world I want! What do you think? Let's vote on it! Come on! Vote for a good world! A better world! A new world! And above all – vote for Mr. –

(He twists his neck, looks behind him at the banner.)

McCrocodile! There! That's all I have to say. Thank you.

("Jerusalem" climaxes.)

*(Wild applause. **HANNAY** looks delighted and bows. Pamela steps forward.)*

PAMELA. This is the man you want inspector!

HANNAY. Where have I heard those words before?

(He makes a bolt for it. The heavies give chase. At last they grab him. Pin him down. Pull him up.)

Scene Twenty-Two: Assembly Hall. Foyer.

(The HEAVIES *drag* HANNAY *to* PAMELA.*)*

HEAVY 1. He's the one, miss?

PAMELA. Yes definitely. He's the one.

HANNAY. I suppose you think you've been damn clever!

PAMELA. Officer kindly tell your prisoner not to insult me
please!

HEAVY 2. Come along now sir!

HANNAY. Don't you see I was speaking the truth in that railway carriage! You must have seen I was genuine!

HEAVY 1. That'll be all ma'am and thank you for your help.

PAMELA. Don't mention it. Goodbye officers.

(The HEAVIES *start to pull* HANNAY *out.)*

HANNAY. Alright just listen please! You have to! There's an
enormously important secret –

HEAVY 2. That'll do now!

HANNAY. – being taken out of this country by a devilishly
brilliant foreign agent! I can't do anything myself
because of these fool detectives! But if you telephone
Scotland Yard immediately and tell them this –

PAMELA. Goodbye, Mr. Hannay!

HEAVY 1. Actually beg pardon, Miss – er –

PAMELA. Edwards. Pamela Edwards.

HEAVY 1. – on second thoughts Miss Edwards we should
like you to come, too.

PAMELA. Me? Whatever for?

HEAVY 2. To identify the prisoner, Miss.

PAMELA. But I've told you who he –

HEAVY 1. Just to the police station Miss.

HEAVY 2. If you wouldn't mind miss.

PAMELA. Well, where is the police station?

HEAVY 1. Inverary, Miss.

PAMELA. Inverary!! But that's nearly –

HANNAY. Forty miles.

PAMELA. *FORTY MILES!?*

HEAVY 1. You keep out of this!

HEAVY 2. He's to be questioned by the Procurator Fiscal personally miss.

PAMELA. Procurator Fiscal personally?

HEAVY 2. It's essential for public security miss.

PAMELA. Essential for public security?

HEAVY 2. That's right miss.

PAMELA. Well if it's absolutely necessary!

HEAVY 1. Thank you miss. If you'd like to climb into the car please miss?

PAMELA. The what?

*(The **CLOWNS** look at each other. They realize they've forgotten the car. **HANNAY** the actor sighs. The **CLOWNS** hastily improvise a car out of chairs, armchair, whatever's to hand.)*

HEAVY 1. The car, miss.

*(**HEAVY 1** starts the motor. **HEAVY 2** gets in beside him. **HANNAY** and **PAMELA** sit behind them. **HANNAY** gives **PAMELA** a delighted grin. Sticks his pipe in his mouth.)*

HANNAY. Hello!

*(**PAMELA** scowls.)*

I'm Richard by the way.

PAMELA. I'm not talking to you.

HANNAY. Right.

(They look out of their respective windows.)

Scene Twenty-Three: Police Car. Night.

*(Car motoring noises. The tyres screech. Occasional lights flash on their faces. **HANNAY** drops off. Nods annoyingly on **PAMELA**'s shoulder.)*

(Suddenly she spots something. Calls out.)

PAMELA. Wait a minute! This is the wrong road! This is the road south. Inverary's north surely.

*(**HANNAY** wakes with a start.)*

HEAVY 2. There's a bridge fallen down on that road, Miss. We shall have to go round. The man knows the way, Miss.

HANNAY. Excuse me, Inspector?

HEAVY 1. What?

HANNAY. Might I see your warrant?

HEAVY 1. You shut your mouth!

*(**HANNAY** whistles the Mr. Memory theme.)*

HANNAY. Would you like to have a small bet with me Pamela?

*(**PAMELA** sighs.)*

Alright, I'll have it with you Sherlock. I'll lay you a hundred to one that your Procurator Fiscal has the top joint of his little finger missing.

*(**HEAVY 1** turns and whacks **HANNAY**. **PAMELA** gasps. **HANNAY** rubs his face and grins.)*

I win.

(The car brakes screech.)

PAMELA. What are we stopping for?

(The car lurches to a halt.)

Scene Twenty-Four: Police Car/Moor.

(Wind. Bleating sheep sounds.)

HEAVY 2. Damned sheep! Get oota the way!

HANNAY. Well, well. A whole flock of detectives.

HEAVY 2. Well, there's nothing else for it. We'll have to clear them away.

HEAVY 1. *(spooked)* Strange they have no shepherd.

HEAVY 2. Come along man!

HEAVY 1. Not so easy in all this thick fog. Look how it's suddenly come down.

(Fog comes down.)

Out of nowhere.

HEAVY 2. *(jumping out of the car)* I said come on man!

HEAVY 1. What about him?

(HEAVY 2 thinks a moment. Unlocks HANNAY's handcuff. Locks it on to PAMELA. HANNAY and PAMELA are now handcuffed together.)

PAMELA. What on earth are you doing! Unchain this handcuff!

HEAVY 2. There you are, Miss. Now you're a special constable. As long as you stay – he stays!

(to HEAVY 1)

Come on! Clear the road!

(to sheep) Get off the road ye mangey beasts!

HEAVY 1. Awa' awa' ye bleating brutes!

(They chase away the sheep and exit.)

HANNAY. And as long as I go – you go! *COME ON!*

(He jumps out of the car, pipe between his teeth. Pulls PAMELA with him.)

PAMELA. What are you doing!

HANNAY. Now you listen to me!

(Takes the pipe out of his mouth. Sticks it in her back.)

Feel this – *pistol?*

PAMELA. Yes!

HANNAY. Do you want me to shoot you stone dead?

PAMELA. Not particularly no.

HANNAY. Then get a move on!

(**HANNAY** *pushes her out. They exit.*)

(*The two* **HEAVIES** *run back in. See the empty car.*)

HEAVY 2. They got away!

HEAVY 1. Where'd they go!?

HEAVY 2. How do I know!? If we don't find them –

HEAVY 1. Yes?

HEAVY 2. – our lives wont be worth living!

HEAVY 1. Oh my God!

(**HEAVY 1** *starts to run out.* **HEAVY 2** *pulls him back.*)

HEAVY 2. Wait wait!

HEAVY 1. What what?

HEAVY 2. The car the car!

HEAVY 1. Where? Where?

HEAVY 2. There! There!

(*He piles the chairs, armchair or whatever was used for the car onto* **HEAVY 1**.)

Take it take it!!

HEAVY 1. I'm taking it I'm taking it!

HEAVY 2. Gotta find 'em! Gotta find 'em!

HEAVY 1. Gotta find 'em! Gotta find 'em!

HEAVY 2. I just said that!

HEAVY 1. I know you just said that!

HEAVY 2. Well don't say it again!

HEAVY 1. Alright! Alright!

HEAVY 2. Now come on come on!

HEAVY 1. Come on come on!

(**CLOWN 2** *charges out, leaving* **CLOWN 1** *loaded wth the car.* **CLOWN 1** *totters off stage. There is a deafening crash as he drops the car in the wings.*)

Scene Twenty-Five: The Dark Moors.

(HANNAY *appears with* PAMELA. *They are handcuffed together as they cross the dark moors. He is pulling her after him.*)

HANNAY. Come on!

(PAMELA *sinks in a bog.*)

PAMELA. I'm stuck! I can't move!

HANNAY. Yes you can!

(HANNAY *pulls at her handcuff. Pulls her out.*)

PAMELA. Ow!!!

(calls out)

Help!

HANNAY. *(pushes his hidden pipe into her ribs again)* Listen! One more peep out of you, I'll shoot you first and myself after. I mean it! Now come on!

PAMELA. Now I'm in a puddle!

HANNAY. So you are.

(He pulls her out. She shrieks.)

PAMELA. I'm soaked through!

HANNAY. I never said it'd be easy Pamela, my dear.

(takes deep breath)

Smell that heather! Makes you glad to be alive doesn't it!

PAMELA. Lovely, yes.

HANNAY. Come on!

(He pulls her after him.)

PAMELA. Will you stop doing that!

(He starts to whistle Mr. Memory Theme.)

And do stop whistling! Look what are you doing all this for? You can't possibly escape! What chance have you got, tied to me?

HANNAY. Keep that question for your husband if I were you.

PAMELA. I don't have a husband!

HANNAY. Lucky him! Come along!

(whistles again)

What IS that tune! Right. Under this stile.

PAMELA. *Ow!*

(He drags her under a stile. She gets jammed. He comes tries to help. She gets more jammed. Now he gets jammed. They become entwined. All the while they banter away.)

HANNAY. We seem a little stuck.

PAMELA. Is that so?

HANNAY. Hang on.

PAMELA. What?

HANNAY. If you go – then if I go – no that doesn't work – wait a minute – let's start again –

PAMELA. I say what is the use of all this?

*(**HANNAY** pulls. **PAMELA** squeaks.)*

Ow!

*(**HANNAY** whistles.)*

And please stop whistling! Those policemen will get you as soon as it's light you know, as soon as daybreak dawns.

HANNAY. They're not policemen.

PAMELA. Oh really? So when did you find that out?

HANNAY. You found it out yourself. I'd never have known that was the wrong road to Inverary! They were taking us to their boss with the little finger missing and God help either of us if we meet him!

PAMELA. So you're still sticking to your penny novelette spy story!

(They are now completely entwined. He rounds on her.)

HANNAY. Listen!

PAMELA. Ow!

HANNAY. There are twenty million women in this island and I've got to be chained to you! I'll say it one more time. There's a dangerous conspiracy against this island and we're the only people who can stop it!

PAMELA. The gallant knight to the rescue!

HANNAY. Alright then you're alone on a desolate moor in the dark, manacled to a plain common murderer who stabbed an innocent defenceless woman four days ago and can't wait to get you off his hands! If that's the situation you'd prefer then have it my girl and welcome!

PAMELA. I'm not afraid of you!

(She sneezes.)

Atchoo!

HANNAY. Bless you.

PAMELA. Thank you.

HANNAY. Pleasure.

(For a second they are very close. They gaze at one another. They wonder what to do. He pulls her through the stile and wrenches her up. PAMELA squeals.)

PAMELA. OW!! You're horrible!!! You just don't care do you! You just walk into my life and look at me! I'm cold and I'm wet and I'm miserable and my wrist hurts and I didn't do anything to hurt you! You're utterly horrid and beastly and heartless! You don't care about anything except your pompous, selfish, horrible, heartless self!

(The wind rages. HANNAY looks at her. She looks at him.)

HANNAY. Yes well, that's the kind of man I am, I'm afraid.

PAMELA. Well, God help your wife, that's all I can say!

HANNAY. Yes, God help her!

(They stand miserably chained together in the wind.)

(Scottish pipe music)

(A flickering neon-lit sign rather majestically flies in through the mist. "THE McGARRIGLE HOTEL – A Warm Welcome Awaits Ye!")

(The "O" on "HOTEL" has fused.)

(Through the dry ice **CLOWN 2** *in kilt and Highland garb mimes the bagpipes.)*

(On the other side **CLOWN 1** *appears as* **MRS MCGAR-RIGLE,** *pushing on the Hotel reception desk.)*

*(***CLOWN 2** *puts down his bagpipes and joins her as* **MR. MCGARRIGLE.***)*

Scene Twenty Six: McGarrigle Hotel

(MR & MRS MCGARRIGLE *listen wide-eyed to the raging wind outside.*)

MRS MCGARRIGLE. It's a terrible Highland night, Willy!

MR MCGARRIGLE. Aye.

MRS MCGARRIGLE. All that rain and wind rushing down the glen! Wouldn't want to be out alone tonight!

MR MCGARRIGLE. No.

HANNAY. *(off)* Hellooo!

(*The* MCGARRIGLES *start.*)

MRS MCGARRIGLE. Did ye hear that?

MR MCGARRIGLE. Aye.

HANNAY. *(off)* Hellooo!

MRS MCGARRIGLE. There it goes again!

(HANNAY *and* PAMELA *enter. She is even more soaking and bedraggled than ever.*)

Ach, ye poor dears! Look Willy. It's a young couple come outta the night! Come away in sir, come away in! Ach dear the poor young lassie's terrible wet! My poor wee dears!

HANNAY. Thanks awfully! We had an accident with our car a few miles back.

MRS MCGARRIGLE. *(with strong accent)* Have ye no luggage?

HANNAY. Sorry?

MRS MCGARRIGLE. Have ye no luggage?

(HANNAY *stares back blankly.*)

MR MCGARRIGLE. Have ye no luggage?

HANNAY. Oh yes! Of course! It's – in the car.

MRS MCGARRIGLE. In the car, of course. Anyway welcome to the McGarrigle Hotel. I am Mrs McGarrigle. This is my husband Willie McGarrigle.

MR MCGARRIGLE. Aye.

HANNAY. How do you do. Anyway –

MRS MCGARRIGLE. You can be certain that at the McGarrigle Hotel a warm McGarrigle welcome awaits ye.

HANNAY. Thank you. As I was –

MRS MCGARRIGLE. Isn't that right, Willie?

MR MCGARRIGLE. Aye.

HANNAY. Marvellous. Anyway –

MRS MCGARRIGLE. Despite it being off-season.

HANNAY. Yes. Um we'd like to stay the night if you could accommodate us.

MRS MCGARRIGLE. Ach well! Let us see. Let us see. Let us see.

(peers at book)

Well – we've just the one bedroom left. With the – er – one bed in it.

*(She beams cheekily. **PAMELA** freezes.)*

But ye'll not be minding that?

HANNAY. No no. Quite the reverse!

MRS MCGARRIGLE. You are man and wife I suppose?

HANNAY. Oh yes.

*(nudges **PAMELA**)*

PAMELA. Er…yes.

MRS MCGARRIGLE. *(beaming)* I thought ye were! I thought ye were! If ye would ne mind registering please? Willie the book.

MR MCGARRIGLE. Ay!

*(**MR MCGARRIGLE** opens the Guest Book.)*

HANNAY. Thank you.

*(He tries to write in the register but realises his right hand is chained to **PAMELA**'s left.)*

Ah! Um, can't actually write with my right hand. Got a bit er –

MR MCGARRIGLE. Bruised?

HANNAY. Sorry?

MR MCGARRIGLE. Cranking the car?

HANNAY. Cranking the car! Quite right! Tell you what? Why don't you sign my darling? The sooner you get used to writing your new name the better. Remember what it is?

PAMELA. No.

HANNAY. Yes I think you do actually, don't you darling?

(He presses the stem of his pipe into her back. PAMELA flinches.)

Mr. and Mrs. Henry Hopkinson –

(PAMELA writes. MR & MRS MCGARRIGLE beam away as she does so.)

– Hollyhocks – *(he thinks)* – Hammersmith – *(he thinks)* – Hampshire.

(PAMELA finishes.)

HANNAY. Well done darling.

MRS. MCGARRIGLE. And there we are!

HANNAY. So anyway I think we'll be – er –

MRS MCGARRIGLE. *(very fast)* Will ye be needing yer suppers?

HANNAY. Sorry?

MRS MCGARRIGLE. Will ye be needing yer suppers?

(awkward pause)

MR MCGARRIGLE. Will you be needing your suppers!

HANNAY. Oh yes! Splendid. Thank you. If you could send up a large whisky and soda and a few sandwiches. Oh and a glass of milk.

MRS MCGARRIGLE. Of course of course! Ach the young doves. Would you care to follow me to your room now please?

HANNAY. Certainly. Darling?

(PAMELA resists. HANNAY pokes the pipe into her back. Together they follow the MCGARRIGLES.)

Scene Twenty-Seven: Hotel Bedroom.

(MRS MCGARRIGLE leads them into their room.)

MRS MCGARRIGLE. There we are now. All ready for ye. A fine roaring fire! *(A burning log fire starts to flicker. A few seconds too late. They all wait till it lights.)*

HANNAY. Marvellous!

(They all rub their hands.)

MRS MCGARRIGLE. Now dearie off with that wet skirt of yours and I'll have it dried in the kitchen.

PAMELA. No don't worry. It'll dry by the fire just as well thanks all the same.

MRS MCGARRIGLE. No doubt the gentleman will take good care of you.

(beams naughtily)

Goodnight sir. Goodnight madam.

HANNAY. Goodnight.

(He nudges PAMELA.)

PAMELA. Goodnight.

(MRS MCGARRIGLE leaves, closing the door gently behind her.)

(PAMELA rounds on HANNAY.)

PAMELA. Look! If you think I'm going to spend the whole night with you in this room! In that –

HANNAY. What else are you going to do?

PAMELA. *(wrenches at her handcuff)* Let me go!

(Knock knock on the door.)

(HANNAY pulls PAMELA over to a chair. Sits her on his knee.)

HANNAY. Come in.

(MRS MCGARRIGLE appears carrying a tray of over-large sandwiches, a glass of whisky and tumbler of milk. Assumes they are cuddling. Looks coyly at the ground.)

MRS MCGARRIGLE. Och, excuse me!

HANNAY. It's quite alright. We were just getting warm by the fire.

(nudges her)

Weren't we darling?

PAMELA. What?

HANNAY. Weren't we darling?

PAMELA. Yes.

HANNAY. Darling.

PAMELA. *Darling!*

MRS MCGARRIGLE. I can see that. Anyway here's your wee sandwiches, your whisky and your glass of milk.

HANNAY. Thank you.

MRS MCGARRIGLE. Will there be anything else?

HANNAY. No thank you.

PAMELA. *I say please don't go!*

(Everyone freezes.)

MRS MCGARRIGLE. Why ever not? Is anything wrong?

HANNAY. Of course there's nothing wrong. She wants to tell you something that's all.

(thinking fast)

We're a runaway couple.

MRS MCGARRIGLE. Och! I ken'd it all the time.

HANNAY. Sorry?

MRS MCGARRIGLE. I ken'd it all the time.

(slight pause)

HANNAY. Anyway you won't give us away will you?

MRS MCGARRIGLE. Of course we won't give you away! You're secret's safe with us. Ye'll nae be disturbed.

(Tiptoes out coyly. Pamela scowls.)

HANNAY. Come along tuck in! What do you want?

(looks inside sandwiches)

Ham and tomato or – ham and tomato?

PAMELA. Ham and tomato.

HANNAY. Ham and tomato. Then I'll have – ham and tomato.

(They wolf down the sandwiches.)

Listen you better get that skirt off!

PAMELA. I beg your pardon?

HANNAY. I Don't want to be tied to a pneumonia case on top of everything else! Take it off, I don't mind!

PAMELA. I shall keep it on thank you!

(They chomp away in silence. The wind moans outside)

Actually, I will take my shoes off.

(She takes her shoes off, his hand dangling by hers. They both eat away while she does this,)

And my stockings.

(He says nothing. She looks at him. Tentatively lifts her skirt to the suspenders of one thigh. She tries to undo the suspenders, still holding the sandwich.)

HANNAY. Can I be of assistance?

PAMELA. No thank you.

HANNAY. Alright.

(She tries again. Gives up.)

PAMELA. Hold this.

(She gives him her sandwich. She lifts her skirt again and undoes the suspender. He does not look.)

(music)

(She rolls the stocking all the way down to her ankle and glides it off. His hand trails lightly with hers. Neither says a word. We become aware of the wind buffeting the window. The crackling fire in the grate. Now she lifts her skirt on the other thigh. Flicks open the suspenders. Starts to roll down the stocking. Once again his hand trails lightly along beside hers, down her thigh, over her knee, down her shin to her ankle. She glides it off. Once again neither says a word. She gets up. He follows her. She hangs the stockings in front of the fire. One falls. He picks it up.)

HANNAY. Here.

PAMELA. Thank you.

HANNAY. Would you like your milk now?

PAMELA. Thank you.

(He gives it to her. She drinks her milk. He drinks his whisky.)

HANNAY. Warmer now?

PAMELA. Yes thanks.

(They stand looking at the fire.)

HANNAY. Well come along.

(He leads her to the bed. She follows compliantly for a moment. Then stops suddenly.)

PAMELA. What are you doing!!?

HANNAY. Going to bed.

PAMELA. *Certainly not! I am not lying on that bed!*

HANNAY. So long as you're chained to me, you lie where I lie. Sorry.

*(***PAMELA*** looks round the room. Realises there's nowhere else. Sighs loudly and clambers on to the bed, pulling him after her. They lie down awkwardly.)*

PAMELA. I want you to know I hate you!

HANNAY. Right.

(She tries to turn away from him. The handcuffs pull her back.)

PAMELA. Ow!

(Grudgingly she lies on her side facing him. She closes her eyes. Tries to sleep.)

*(***HANNAY*** starts humming again.)*

*(***PAMELA*** opens her eyes crossly.)*

PAMELA. Will you stop *doing* that!

HANNAY. There I go again! I wish I could get that damn tune out of my head. I wonder where I heard it?

(yawns loudly)

HANNAY. D'you know when I last slept in a bed? Saturday night. Whenever that was. Then I only got a couple of hours.

PAMELA. What woke you? Dreams? I imagine murderers have terrible dreams.

HANNAY. Oh I used to. I used to wake up in the middle of the night screaming. Thinking the police were after me. Funny that! You see when I first took to a life of crime, I was quite squeamish about it. A most sensitive child.

(yawns)

PAMELA. You do surprise me.

HANNAY. But I soon got hardened. Before long I was an out and out villain. Wanted on three continents.

*(He yawns again. He starts to snore. **PAMELA** surreptitiously pulls their chained wrists towards her. He wakes.)*

Just think in years to come, you'll be able to take your grandchildren to Madame Tussauds and point me out.

PAMELA. Which section?

HANNAY. Inveterate, unreformable no-hopers. Wedded to a life of crime. That's me, Pamela my darling. And the sad story of my life. Poor little orphan boy who never had a chance. Irredeemable. Irreclaimable.

(yawns)

Utterly horrid and beastly.

(She gazes at him. He mutters away with closed eyes.)

I'd get away from me as quick as you can if I was you.

(yawns)

Oh no, you can't, can you.?

(yawns)

Oh well…

(He snores loudly. She gazes down at him tenderly for a moment. Then pulls herself together. Begins to twist on her handcuff. Painfully jiggling, she inches the handcuff over her wrist. At last she wrenches it off. She lays

the empty handcuff beside **HANNAY**. *With a groan he rolls over and embraces her in sleep. She gasps. Gently lifts his arm and puts it back. Slides silently off the bed. Crosses the room, thinks of something. Puts her hand in his pocket. Takes out his pipe. Slams it crossly on the table. Tip-toes to the door and slips out.)*

Scene Twenty-Eight: Hotel Lobby. Night.

(The two **HEAVIES** *are revealed at the reception desk. One is talking urgently into the phone.)*

HEAVY 2. Mrs. Jordan! Please listen! We *had* to take the girl as well!

*(***MRS JORDAN*** voice shrieks indecipherably on the phone [Sound or actor's own voice behind hat].)*

Unfortunately not. We lost both her and Hannay, I'm afraid!

(Louder shrieking from **MRS JORDAN.***)*

*(***PAMELA*** appears in the shadows. She listens wide-eyed.)*

He'll have told her the whole plot by now! *She'll know we're not the real police!*

*(***PAMELA*** gasps audibly.)*

(Big shriek from **MRS JORDAN.** **HEAVY 2** *holds phone away from his ear.)*

Dispose of them both when we find them? Certainly Mrs. Jordan!

*(***PAMELA*** claps hand to her mouth.)*

Beg pardon, madam? *Has he? Does he!? Is he?!* Yes indeed, madam! Certainly, madam! Goodbye, madam! Thank you, madam.

(Slams down receiver.)

HEAVY 1. Well? Spill the beans!

HEAVY 2. The professor's got the wind up. He's cleared out already!

HEAVY 1. Cleared out already?

HEAVY 2. Thought it was too dangerous with Hannay and this girl on the loose. He's warning the whole Thirty-Nine Steps.

HEAVY 1. The whole Thirty-Nine Steps? Does he have the – *you know?*

HEAVY 2. Certainly does!

HEAVY 1. Thank God for that!

HEAVY 2. Yes! And he's picking up our friend from the London Palladium! Tonight! On the way out!

HEAVY 1. On the way out! Right.

HEAVY 2. Right! I'll start the car. You check the register.

HEAVY 1. Right.

> (**HEAVY 2** *exits.*)

> (**HEAVY 1** *rings the bell.*)

> (**HEAVY 2** *returns as* **MR MCGARRIGLE** *in his night-shirt.*)

MR MCGARRIGLE. Ay? Can I help ye?

HEAVY 1. Yes I was wondering if you might have happened to have had a young couple staying here–

MR MCGARRIGLE. Might have had had happened to have had have had a mighty young couple staying? Well now you mention it –

HEAVY 1. Yes?

MR MCGARRIGLE. But can I take your coat by the way?

HEAVY 1. Thanks very much.

> (**MR MCG** *starts taking* **HEAVY 1** *'s coat.*)

HEAVY 1. You were saying?

MR MCGARRIGLE. Well, now you mention it, we do have a young –

> (**HEAVY 1** *becomes* **MRS M**. *She shrieks.*)

MRS MCGARRIGLE. *WILLIE!!!*

MR MCGARRIGLE. Aye!!!???

MRS MCGARRIGLE. What are you doing out here!

MR MCGARRIGLE. The gentleman wanted to know –

MRS MCGARRIGLE. Standing there in your night-gown for all the world to see! Put your coat on! And tidy yourself!

> *(dresses him in the Heavy's coat)*

Get in the kitchen man!

MR MCGARRIGLE. Aye!!!

> (**MRS MCG** *jams trilby on* **MR MCG.** *Turning him into* **HEAVY 2.**)

MRS MCGARRIGLE. And as for ye!!! Whoever ye are!!! I'll thank ye to get oota ma hoose! Waking people up all hours of the night! Have ye have no bed to go to?

HEAVY 2. *(backs away, alarmed)* Right. No. Sorry. Thank you.

> (**HEAVY 2** *exits hastily. She shouts after him.*)

MRS MCGARRIGLE. Thank ye and goodnight!

> (**CLOWN 2** *runs back as* **WILLIE** *in his nightgown.*)

MR MCGARRIGLE. And goodnight!

> (*Sound of car roaring away.* **PAMELA** *emerges from the shadows.* **MRS. MCG** *beams sweetly at her. Takes her hand.*)

MRS MCGARRIGLE. Nothing to worry about now dear. Willy?

MR MCGARRIGLE. Ay?

MRS MCGARRIGLE. Ye wouldn'ae give away a dear young couple, would ye?

MR MCGARRIGLE. No!

MRS MCGARRIGLE. Ye old fool ye! To your bed man!

> (*She shoos him off. As he goes,* **PAMELA** *kisses him on the cheek. He turns to the audience and beams.*)

Scene Twenty-Nine: Hotel Bedroom.

(**HANNAY** *sleeps on oblivious.*)

(**PAMELA** *walks in. A changed woman.*)

(*music*)

(*She gazes at him tenderly.*)

(*Lights change. Birdsong.*)

(**HANNAY** *wakes. He notices the empty handcuffs. Leaps off the bed.*)

PAMELA. Morning.

HANNAY. What's the idea! How did you get out of these? Why didn't you run away?

PAMELA. I did. Then just as I was going I – well, I discovered you'd been speaking the truth. So I thought I'd stay.

HANNAY. May I ask what earthquake caused your brain to work at last?

PAMELA. Two policemen came here last night. The ones from the car. I overheard them telephoning. They're not policemen!

HANNAY. I know they're not policemen! I said they weren't policemen!

PAMELA. Sorry.

HANNAY. So what did they say?

PAMELA. Oh – um – yes! A lot of stuff about – something with a number. Um – twenty – thirty…Thirty! Thirty –

HANNAY. Nine!

PAMELA. Thirty Nine! That's right. Thirty-nine –

HANNAY. Steps!!!

PAMELA. *Thirty-nine steps!* How did you know that? Someone's going to warn them!

HANNAY. *WHAT?*

PAMELA. How can you warn steps?

HANNAY. Never mind. Go on!

PAMELA. Um – yes! There was another thing. Someone's – got the wind up and is – clearing out! And – and – I know! They're picking someone up from the London Palladium!

HANNAY. London Palladium? London Palladium? Who's that, I wonder? Is that the Professor? Our friend with the little finger missing? What's he want to go there for? Funny thing for a master-spy to do!

(They smile at each other. They look at the floor.)

(Romantic music.)

PAMELA. I'm sorry. I feel such an awful fool for not having believed you.

HANNAY. That's alright. Well –

PAMELA. Well –

HANNAY. – we ought to be –

PAMELA. Yes –

HANNAY. – going I suppose.

PAMELA. Mmm.

(They are rather close. Neither moves.)

HANNAY. Right. Um –

PAMELA. Yes?

HANNAY. Which –

PAMELA. What?

HANNAY. – room are they staying in?

PAMELA. Who?

HANNAY. What?

PAMELA. Who?

HANNAY. Those two men?

PAMELA. Sorry?

(They get closer and closer.)

HANNAY. The two men you overheard.

PAMELA. Staying in?

HANNAY. Mmm.

PAMELA. Well, they're not.

HANNAY. Sorry?

PAMELA. They went away as soon as they'd telephoned. They drove off into the night. Rather fast actually.

HANNAY. *(Hardly listening. About to kiss her.)* Where?

PAMELA. Where? Don't know. Sorry.

(Closes her eyes.)

Does it matter?

(His lips are touching hers. Suddenly his eyes snap open. He looks at her. Realizes what's happening.)

HANNAY. *DOES IT MATTER!!!???*

(Music cuts out.)

PAMELA. *What?*

(He leaps up.)

HANNAY. *WHAT DO YOU MEAN DOES IT MATTER!!!???*

PAMELA. I'm sorry I –

HANNAY. You button-headed little idiot! Why didn't you stop them!?

PAMELA. What?

HANNAY. This is unbelievably appalling!

PAMELA. *(examining her head)* Button-headed?

HANNAY. Oh my God!

PAMELA. Sorry!!

HANNAY. Why didn't you stop them for God's sake!

PAMELA. Because I wanted to see you!!

HANNAY. Well that was a stupid thing to do wasn't it!!!

PAMELA. Apparently yes!!!

HANNAY. So where did they go?

PAMELA. I don't know! The London Palladium I suppose!!

HANNAY. The London Palladium? When?

PAMELA. Tonight! On the way out!

HANNAY. On the way out? On the way out of what?!

PAMELA. I don't know what!!!

HANNAY. Well that's four or five precious hours wasted!

PAMELA. Well – well – if they're all leaving the country that's fine isn't it? Just leave well alone!

HANNAY. Leave well alone! Leave well alone! I am accused of murder! The only way to clear my name is to expose these spies!

PAMELA. There you go again you see! *Selfish selfish selfish selfish!!!*

HANNAY. What?

PAMELA. *Heartless, beastly, horrid and selfish!!!*

HANNAY. But *MUCH* more important than that! Much more important than *clearing my name!* They are about to leave the country with a secret vital to the safety of our air defense!

PAMELA. *WELL I'M VERY VERY SORRY!!!*

HANNAY. *WHICH SHOW MATINEE OR EVENING!!!*

PAMELA. *I DON'T KNOW!!!*

HANNAY. *WELL THANKS FOR YOUR HELP! GOODBYE!!!*

PAMELA. *GOODBYE!!!*

(**HANNAY** *marches to the door.*)

HANNAY. *GOODBYE!!!*

PAMELA. *AND DON'T EXPECT ME TO COME WITH YOU!!!*

(**HANNAY** *marches back to her.*)

HANNAY. *I WON'T!!!*

PAMELA. *GOOD!!!*

HANNAY. *GOOD!!!*

(**HANNAY** *exits furiously.*)

PAMELA. *I'M NOT SURPRISED YOU'RE AN ORPHAN!!!*

(*She bursts into tears.*)

Scene Thirty. London Palladium Stage.

(Music: "Sunday Night at the London Palladium" theme.)

ANNOUNCER. This is the London Palladium!

(Tabs fly in. A front cloth act is in full swing.) [3]

(HANNAY appears in the audience. A changed man from the first HANNAY. Exhausted, harrowed, on the run but full of fire and heart. He tries to look normal. Takes out a pair of binoculars. Scans the theatre. Stops suddenly. Trains the binoculars on a stage box.)

(There in a spotlight is a false hand holding a black cigarette holder. A coil of drifting smoke.) [4]

(PAMELA appears in the light behind HANNAY.)

PAMELA. Hello.

(HANNAY spins round.)

HANNAY. Good Lord! Thought you'd run off.

PAMELA. You ran off!

HANNAY. Well I was bloody furious.

(She turns to go.)

PAMELA. I'll go then, shall I?

HANNAY. No no – stay now you're here.

(They hold each other's gaze. Smile.)

PAMELA. Alright.

HANNAY. But now look here! I've found him!

PAMELA. Who?

HANNAY. The professor.

---

3. The nature of the act is the choice of the clowns. A singer, a whistler, a tumbling act, comedy dance act. Something musical or non-verbal. A moment's light relief before the story reaches its climax.

4. In an ideal world, Clown 2 should appear as the professor in the box each time he is mentioned. Without the need for false arms or cigarette-holders. This will depend entirely on your design, amount of wing space and the actor's level of Olympian fitness. Quite a lot of this show depends on your actors' level of Olympian fitness. It has proved an invaluable aid to weight loss.

PAMELA. The professor! Where?

HANNAY. There! In that box. Do you see?

(Spot up on false hand and cigarette-holder.)[5]

PAMELA. Gosh, yes!

(remembers)

But wait a minute?

HANNAY. What?

PAMELA. You can't do anything about it! I've been to Scotland Yard.

HANNAY. *Scotland Yard!?*

PAMELA. My uncle's chief commissioner, actually.

HANNAY. Chief commissioner?

PAMELA. Yes. Uncle Bob.

HANNAY. Uncle Bob?

PAMELA. Yes.

HANNAY. Bob's your uncle?

PAMELA. Yes. And he said nothing's been stolen from the air ministry. No Top Secret information or anything!

HANNAY. But you heard those men say the professor's got it!

PAMELA. Well they've checked and they're absolutely certain.

*(**HANNAY** looks round with his binoculars. Members of the company appear in police helmets.)*

HANNAY. *(springs back)* POLICE! What are the police doing here? They didn't follow you here did they?

PAMELA. Oh dear. Sorry.

HANNAY. *That's it then. That's it!*

*(**COMPERE** enters through the tabs. Bows.)*

(applause)

COMPERE. Good evenin' Ladies and Gentlemen. And now with your kind attention I have the immense honour and privelege to presentin' to you one of the most remarkable men ever in the whole world. Mr. Memory!!!

---

5. See Note 4.

(Music: Mr. Memory Theme)

HANNAY. Wait a minute! That's the damn tune I couldn't get out of my head!

(On comes MR MEMORY. *Canned applause.* COMPERE *exits.)*

HANNAY. *Mr. Memory!*

MR MEMORY. Thankoo. Thankoo. I will now place myself in a state of mental readiness for this evenin's performance and clear my inner bein' of all extinstrinsic and supermernumary material.

(Takes deep breath. Closes his eyes.)

(Drumroll)

*(*MR MEMORY *surreptitiously opens an eye and looks up at the spot-lit box. The professor appears from behind the drape. He makes a coded signal to* MR MEMORY. HANNAY *swings his binoculars to the box, back to* MR MEMORY. MR MEMORY *nods to the box.* HANNAY *gasps triumphantly.)*

HANNAY. *I've got it! I'VE GOT IT!* Of course they don't know anything's missing! All the information's in Memory's head! That's why the professor's here tonight. To take Memory out of the country.

(Drumrolls ends.)

MR MEMORY: Thankoo! Thankoo! First question please!!

(He points into audience.)

Beg pardon sir? Who built St. Paul's Cathedral? Who built St. Paul's Cathedral? Sir Christopher Wren built St. Paul's Cathedral. He done it in the year sixteen sixty –

*(*CHIEF INSPECTOR ALBRIGHT *enters down an aisle.)*

ALBRIGHT. Sorry to disturb the show Ladies and Gents.

*(*MR MEMORY *stops mid-flow.)*

*(*ALBRIGHT *scans audience. He spots* HANNAY.*)*

Richard Charles Arbuthnot Hannay? I am Detective Chief Inspector Albright sir. New Scotland Yard sir. I am arresting you on a charge of *MURDER!*

PAMELA. But you don't understand Detective Chief Inspector Albright!

ALBRIGHT. I think I do, miss. Now come along quietly, sir. There's a good chap, sir.

HANNAY. *(stands bravely)* Alright alright Albright.

PAMELA. He's innocent I tell you!

HANNAY. I'm sorry Pamela there's – no other way!

ALBRIGHT. *(looks smug)* Very wise, sir. Now if you'd just –

(HANNAY vanishes. ALBRIGHT spins round.)

Hannay! He's escaped! QUICK!

(calls out)

Block all the exits! Block all the exits!

(to **MEMORY***)*

Carry on as normal please sir.

MEMORY. Thank you sir. Right sir.

(ALBRIGHT rushes out in hot pursuit. All the ushers follow him blowing their whistles.)

As I was sayin' before bein' interrupted in my flow, Sir Christopher Wren built St. Paul's Cathedral. He done it in the year sixteen sixty –

(HANNAY reappears onstage. Shouts at **MEMORY***.)*

HANNAY. *WHAT ARE THE THIRTY-NINE STEPS?*

(MR MEMORY freezes.)

MEMORY. Sixteen-sixty –

HANNAY. *I SAID WHAT ARE THE THIRTY-NINE STEPS?*

(MR MEMORY catatonic. Terror fills his face.)

HANNAY. Come on man! Answer up!

(MR MEMORY looks up at the professor's box in blind panic. Looks at **HANNAY***. Looks out front. Mops his brow, trembling.)*

MR MEMORY. The…the…the Thirty-Nine Steps sir?

HANNAY. Yes Mr Memory! For the last time! *WHAT ARE THE THIRTY-NINE STEPS?*

(**MR MEMORY** *clicks into automatic. He turns to the audience.*)

MR MEMORY. The Thirty-Nine Steps is an organisation of spies. They collect information on behalf of the Secret Service of –

(*The* **PROFESSOR** *appears in the box.*)

the Secret Service of –

(*The* **PROFESSOR** *takes out a gun. Shoots* **MEMORY**. **MEMORY** *clutches his heart and sinks to the ground.* **HANNAY** *points at the* **PROFESSOR**.)

HANNAY. There! That's the man you want Detective Chief Inspector!!

(*The* **PROFESSOR** *realizes he is exposed. He swings the gun on to* **HANNAY**. *Snarls like a trapped animal.*)

PROFESSOR. I don't think so, Hannay! No no! This is not *your* story. This is *my* story! And I decide how it ends. You don't destroy me, Hannay! And you don't get the girl! Oh no! You lose the girl! You lose the girl and you die of grief! All alone in your dull little rented Portland Place flat! You thought you found love, Hannay? Really? Afraid not old sport! You will never find it you see. Never in all eternity! Sorry!

(*The* **PROFESSOR** *swings the gun back to* **PAMELA**. **PAMELA** *screams Fay Wray style.*)

PAMELA. *Richard! Richard!*

(*But* **HANNAY** *is nowhere to be seen. She looks desperately round for him. Suddenly he appears is in the professor's box.*)

HANNAY. Oh no you don't, Professor!

(**HANNAY** *and the* **PROFESSOR** *wrestle in the box. Round and round they go. They battle for the gun.*)

(*A shot rings out.* **PAMELA** *shrieks. Both men stare at each other. At last the* **PROFESSOR** *gasps and totters. He disappears behind the curtain. He reappears doing ever* *more extravagant death throes. At the last moment he hurls a replica dummy of himself out of the box into the audience.)*

(canned screams)

(MR MEMORY *is sinking on stage. Bravely keeping the show going.)*

MR MEMORY. Keep your seats please! No need for panic ladies and gentlemen! Bring on the dancing girls! Stay calm! Stay calm!

(Dancing Girls music.)

(The Tabs fly out, to reveal…)

Scene Thirty-One. London Palladium. Backstage.

(HANNAY *and* PAMELA *run on with the* COMPERE.
They kneel beside MR MEMORY. MR. MEMORY *is fading
fast.*)

COMPERE. Take it easy, old chap. There's a good chap.

MR MEMORY. Just a scratch, Bert. I'll be alright.

(*He winces.*)

HANNAY. Mr. Memory?

MR MEMORY. Yes sir?

HANNAY. What was the secret formula you were taking out
of the country?

MR MEMORY. Will it be alright me telling you, sir?

HANNAY. It will, Mr. Memory.

MR MEMORY. It was a big job to learn it, sir. The biggest job
I ever had to tackle! And I don't want to throw it all
away, sir.

HANNAY. Of course not old man.

MR MEMORY. The first feature of the new engine is its greatly
increased ratio of compression, represented by r minus
1 over r to the power of gamma and 9 sequenced to the
power of xy squared duplicated by 32 point, 71 point
and 88 point recurring reduced by 19 alpha providing
equal cubes of epsilon in serial circumference aligned
to three double governor valves flowing radially to the
point of 3/65pi – arranged in series –

(*He gasps, fades. They bow their heads. He revives.*)

– with concentric rows of blading, alternating with
fixed rows on the diaphragms. The longtitudinal pressure exerted on the turbine shafts is counterbalanced
by a grooved piston at the HP end of the shaft, excess
pressure being taken by the adjustable thrust block
which locates the rotor to the power of 900abh/7 and
seen in end elevation the access of the true line of cyl-
inders is an angle of 65 degrees. This device renders
the engine – completely silent!

(**HANNAY** *gasps as he realizes the full devilishness of the professor's plot.* **MR MEMORY** *gazes up at* **HANNAY**.)

MR MEMORY. *(cont.)* Am I right, sir?

HANNAY. Quite right, old chap.

MR MEMORY. Thank you sir. I'm glad it's off my mind at last, sir.

(**MR MEMORY** *dies.*)

(*The* **COMPERE** *sobs over* **MR MEMORY**'s *body. Lights go down.*)

(**HANNAY** *and* **PAMELA** *revealed at the front of the stage.*)

Scene Thirty-Two. Outside Palladium. Night.

HANNAY. Well…

PAMELA. Well…you're a free man anyway.

HANNAY. Right.

PAMELA. Saved the country too.

HANNAY. We both did that.

PAMELA. Not really.

HANNAY. Anyway…better be um –

PAMELA. Right.

HANNAY. D'you want to –

PAMELA. What?

(**HANNAY** *looks at her. She looks at him.*)

HANNAY. Nothing.

PAMELA. Quite.

HANNAY. Better be going.

PAMELA. Yes.

HANNAY. Got the decorators in and – you know.

PAMELA. Certainly do.

HANNAY. Well – bye.

PAMELA. Bye.

(**PAMELA** *goes.* **HANNAY**'s *face full of regret.*)

Scene Thirty-Three: Hannay's Flat. Night.

(**HANNAY** *walks into his room. Exactly as it was at the beginning. He sits in his armchair.*)

HANNAY. So that's me. And the sad story of my life. Richard Hannay. Irredeemable. Irreclaimable. Unreformable.

(Romantic music)

(**PAMELA** *walks in. She gazes at him.*)

PAMELA. Utterly horrid and beastly.

(She kneels beside him.)

Poor little orphan boy who never had a chance.

(She takes his hand and kisses it.)

This is the man I want inspector.

(A little Christmas tree trundles in. The tree lights up.)

HANNAY. Happy Christmas darling.

PAMELA. Happy Christmas darling.

(A baby cries.)

(**PAMELA** *smiles at* **HANNAY**. *He pulls her towards him. They kiss.*)

(Snow falls at the window.)

The End